HIJACKED—TO ANOTHER GALAXY

The aliens had taken over the Enterprise and were hurtling the ship toward their home galaxy, on a mission that would doom mankind. Their chief was in total command.

"Now, as to bridge personnel . . ." He moved toward Uhura. "We have no need of communications for some centuries."

Uhura sat frozen in her chair, staring at him in horror. He touched his belt device—and there was nothing left in her seat but a geometrical solid, about the size of a fist.

"And since we are now capable of doing our own navigating . . ." Chekov also vanished.

STAR TREK 6

Bantam Books by James Blish
Ask your bookseller for the books you have missed

SPOCK MUST DIE!
STAR TREK 1
STAR TREK 2
STAR TREK 3
STAR TREK 4
STAR TREK 5
STAR TREK 6
STAR TREK 7
STAR TREK 8
STAR TREK 9
STAR TREK 10
STAR TREK 11

STAR TREK 6

JAMES BLISH

Based on the Exciting Television Series
Created by Gene Roddenberry

STAR TREK 6

A Bantam Book / April 1972

2nd printing	*May 1972*	*8th printing*	*September 1974*
3rd printing	*September 1972*	*9th printing*	*November 1975*
4th printing	*November 1972*	*10th printing*	*November 1975*
5th printing	*May 1973*	*11th printing*	*November 1977*
6th printing	*August 1974*	*12th printing*	*April 1979*
7th printing	*September 1974*	*13th printing*	*December 1979*

This book is published by Bantam Books under License from Paramount Pictures Corporation.

ISBN 0-553-13874-X

Published simultaneously in the United States and Canada

Bantam Books are published by Bantam Books, Inc. Its trademark, consisting of the words "Bantam Books" and the portrayal of a bantam, is Registered in U.S. Patent and Trademark Office and in other countries. Marca Registrada. Bantam Books, Inc., 666 Fifth Avenue, New York, New York 10019.

PRINTED IN THE UNITED STATES OF AMERICA

CONTENTS

PREFACE

The fan mail continues to pour in, listing favorite shows, making helpful suggestions and occasionally catching errors. (To reply to one persistent complaint, it was not I who made Kirk address McCoy as "Doc" instead of "Bones" in "Spock Must Die!" I know better than that; but there are several editorial hands laid on the manuscript after mine before it reaches the printer.) I am grateful for them all, including the pats on the back.

One recent letter was so extraordinary, however, that I think it deserves passing on. With permission, I quote the important part of it:

JAMES BLISH

> By an interesting coincidence I happen to be Captain [Pierre D.] Kirk. This being the case, the men of my last command built a rather elaborate "organization within an organization" based on the series. My jeep was slightly altered so that its registration numbers appeared as NCC-1701. Our weapons were referred to as phasers and our radio communication procedures were patterned after those of the Star Fleet. Our call signs corresponded to the various sections and personalities of the crew of the *Enterprise*.
>
> My junior officers picked up the names of the more recognizable regular characters in the series. My

executive officer made an excellent Spock in that he physically as well as temperamentally resembled the Vulcan. The men wanted him to get an "ear job" but he drew the line at this.

As you can see, the men of the 363rd [Transportation Company, U.S. Army] went to some lengths to identify with the Star Trek series. This was quite an effective means to maintain morale in the present unpleasantness in Indochina.

The series, by the way, is one of the most popular shown in the Republic of Viet Nam—a great favorite of both the American forces and the Viet-Namese people.

Turning to the point of this letter—about eight months ago I was in command of an armed convoy en route from An Khe in the central highlands to Da Nang on the Northern coast. As we proceeded along route QL #1, which the late Bernard Fall referred to as "the Street without Joy," we were engaged by snipers, which usually served as the prelude to an ambush.

Deciding to run through the suspected area, I signaled my gun trucks to cover our cargo vehicles, and then via my jeep radio I announced: "Attention Viet Cong. We are the Federation Starship *Enterprise* and you are now in deep trouble. Phaser banks—charge your phasers and fire on my order."

This comment was directed at my gun trucks to serve to fire them up for what promised to be a tight situation, but to my surprise the radio exploded into a torrent of frantic jabbering in Viet-Namese and moments later the sniping ceased and we continued through without incident.

The only thing I can assume is that the V. C. were monitoring our broadcast transmissions, had seen the show on television and thought that we were in fact the *Enterprise*.

Under the circumstances I can readily understand this reluctance to engage us in a fight. Happily I can report that despite their initial sniper activity no casualties were suffered by the crew of the *Enterprise*.

I had heard of other organizations patterned on the show, including an entire high school in Buffalo, N.Y., where disliked teachers are assigned to the Romulans or the Klingons; but this is the first time I have ever heard of a television series actually saving lives (on both sides, for that matter).

Which only goes to show all over again that it pays to read the fan mail, even though I can't answer it.

JAMES BLISH

Harpsden (Henley)
Oxon., England

THE SAVAGE CURTAIN
(Gene Roddenberry and Arthur Heinemann)

The planet, newly discovered in an uncharted area of space, was clearly not a Class M world. The atmosphere boiled with poisonous reds and greens; the surface was molten lava.

And yet, from one small area Spock picked up persistent readings of carbon cycle life forms—and artificial power being generated in quantities great enough to support a considerable civilization. Hailing on all frequencies at first produced nothing . . . and then, suddenly, the *Enterprise* was being scanned, an incredibly swift and deep probe.

Kirk barely had time to call for alert status when the probing was over. Almost immediately afterward, the image of the planet on the main viewing screen dissolved into a swirling jumble of colors. These slowly gathered together into a face and figure, entirely human, dressed in clothing like those worn in the mid-1800's on Earth. He was sitting on nothing and with nothing visible behind him, as though in limbo. His expression was benign and calm.

"Captain Kirk, I believe?" the figure said. "A pleasure to make your acquaintance, sir."

Kirk, Spock and McCoy stared incredulously at the familiar figure. Finally, Kirk motioned to Uhura.

"Your voice-telegraph device is quite unnecessary,

Captain," the figure said. "Do I gather that you recognize me?"

"I . . . recognize what you appear to be."

"And appearances can be quite deceiving." The figure smiled. "But not in this case, James Kirk. I am Abraham Lincoln."

Kirk considered this incredible claim and apparition, and then turned to his First Officer. "Spock?"

"Fascinating, Captain."

"I've been described in many ways, Mr. Spock," the smiling man said, "but never with that word."

"I was requesting your analysis of this, Mr. Spock."

"They did scan us and our vessel," Spock said, "and doubtless obtained sufficient information to present this illusion."

"Illusion?" the figure said. "Captain, will you permit me to come aboard your vessel? No doubt you have devices which can test my reality."

After a moment's hesitation, Kirk said, "We'd be honored to have you aboard, Mr. President."

The figure reached into its vest pocket, pulled out a large watch on a heavy gold chain and snapped the lid open. "Do you still measure time in minutes?"

"Yes, sir."

"Then you should be over my position in . . . twelve and a half minutes. Until then, Captain . . ." The image on the screen rippled, dissolved and re-formed itself as the planet. Amid the hot reds and poisonous greens of the atmosphere there was now a spot of soft blue. Spock leaned into his hooded viewer.

"An area of approximately a thousand square kilometers, sir," he said. "It's completely Earthlike, including an oxygen-nitrogen atmosphere."

"He called it to the second, sir," Chekov added. "We'll be over it in exactly twelve minutes now."

Kirk touched the intercom button. "Security. Send a detachment to the Transport Room immediately. Phaser side arms—but be prepared also to give presidential honors. Captain out."

"Jim," McCoy said, "you don't really believe he's Abraham Lincoln?"

"It's obvious he believes it, Bones." Kirk stood up. "Mr. Spock, Doctor, full dress uniforms, please. Mr. Sulu, the con is yours."

In the Transporter Room, Security Chief Dickenson had assembled two security guards, phasers at port. Dickenson himself sported white boots and belt, plus a traditional bos'n's whistle on a gold chain.

Engineering Officer Scott, in full kilt, entered and moved to the Transporter console, fuming. "Full dress! Presidential honors! What's all this nonsense, Mr. Dickenson?"

"I understand President Lincoln is coming aboard, sir."

Scott whirled. "Are you daft, man?"

"All I know, sir, is what the Captain tells me, sir," Dickenson said uncomfortably. "And he said he'd have the hide of the first man who so much as smiles."

McCoy entered, also in full dress, with his tricorder over his shoulder. Scott eyed him dourly; McCoy gave back stare for stare.

"I'd have expected sanity from the ship's surgeon, at least." Scott irritably punched controls on the console. "President Lincoln, indeed! No doubt followed by Louis of France and Robert the Bruce."

Kirk and Spock had come in in time to catch this last remark.

"And if so, Mr. Scott, we'll execute appropriate honors to each," Kirk said. "Gentlemen, I don't believe for a moment that Abraham Lincoln is actually coming aboard. But we are dealing with an unknown and apparently quite advanced life form. Until we know ... well, when in Rome, we do as the Romans do."

"Bridge to Transporter Room," Chekov's voice said over the intercom. "One minute to overhead position."

"Locking onto something," Scott said. He looked closer, and then gestured at the panel. "Does that appear human to you, Mr. Spock?"

Spock joined him and inspected the console. "Fascinating! . . . For a moment it appeared almost mineral. Like living rock, with heavy fore-claws . . . Settling down into completely human readings now."

"We can beam it aboard any time now, Captain," Scott said.

"Set for traditional ruffles and flourishes. Security, stand ready."

"Phaser team, set for heavy stun," Dickenson said. "Honor guard, ready."

The two security men posted themselves on opposite sides of the Transporter chamber, weapons set, raised and aimed. The four men comprising the honor guard snapped into parade rest. Dickenson raised his whistle to his lips.

"Energize."

The sparkling column appeared, solidified, vanished. The figure left standing there seemed to be inarguably Abraham Lincoln, dressed in the well-remembered 19th century suit, bearded, his face registering the sad wisdom of his presidential years.

Dickenson blew his whistle. Spock pushed a panel button and everyone came to attention. Ruffles and flourishes filled the air.

"Salute!" Kirk said. Everyone did except the two guards, whose phasers remained ready. Lincoln, too, stood gravely at attention through the music. Then Kirk said, "Two!," broke the salute and stepped forward.

"The USS *Enterprise* is honored to have you aboard, Mr. President."

"Strange," Lincoln said, stepping down. "Where are the musicians?"

"Taped music, sir. Starships on detached service do not carry full honor detachments."

"Taped music? Perhaps Mr. Spock will be good enough to explain that to me later." Lincoln extended a hand to Kirk. "A most interesting way to come aboard, Captain. What was the device used?"

"A matter-energy scrambler sir. The molecules of your body were converted to energy, and beamed to this chamber where they were reconverted to their original pattern."

Lincoln hesitated. "Well, since I am obviously here and quite whole, whatever you mean apparently works very well indeed." He looked at the two guards. "If those are weapons, gentlemen, you may lower them. At my age, I'm afraid I'm not very dangerous."

"Readings, fully human, sir," McCoy said.

Kirk signaled the guards to holster their weapons, and then introduced everyone present.

"Please stand at ease, gentlemen," Lincoln said. "I hope to talk to each of you, but meanwhile, your Captain is consumed with questions and I shall do my utmost to answer them. And I trust your duties will permit time to answer some of mine. At your service, Captain."

"Mr. Spock." Kirk led his First Officer and his guest off toward the Briefing Room.

"A marvel," Lincoln said. "A total marvel. I can hardly credit my eyes. We thought our *Monitor* the most formidable vessel imaginable—an iron ship that floated on water! You can imagine my amazement at an iron ship that floats on air."

"Mr. President—"

"Yes, Captain. Forgive my excitement at the novelty of all this."

"Sir . . . I find some of your comments hard to equate with other statements. For example, you are not at all surprised at the existence of this vessel. But you then exhibit only a 19th century knowledge about it—for example, stating that this vessel 'floats on air.'"

"I don't understand. What *does* your vessel float on, captain?"

Kirk exchanged a look with Spock and said patiently, "Sir, the atmosphere surrounding any planet is a relatively thin envelope."

Lincoln appeared genuinely puzzled. Spock went on: "Given our present altitude, sir, and a present speed converting to 19,271 Earth miles per Earth hour, our velocity counterbalances the pull of this planet's gravity, creating equal but opposite forces which maintain us in orbit."

This was quite a distance away from the real physical situation, but Spock had evidently decided to choose terms which might be familiar to a 19th century educated man, rather than having to explain what was meant by free fall through a matter-distorted space-time matrix. But even the simplification did not work.

"When the choice is between honesty and disguising ignorance," Lincoln said, "a wise man chooses the former. I haven't the faintest idea what you said."

"With all respect, sir, that still does not answer my question," Kirk said. "For example, you knew my name. How is it you know some things about us but not others?"

"Bless me! Yes, I do see the contradiction," Lincoln said, frowning. "Please believe I have neither desire nor intention to deceive you, gentlemen. I must have been told these things, but I . . . I cannot recall when or where."

"Can you guess who it might have been, sir?" Spock said. "What others exist on the planet's surface with you?"

"Others? What others do you mean?"

"That's clearly not Earth down there, Mr. President," Kirk said. "Or do you believe that it is?"

"Strange," Lincoln said thoughtfully, "I never considered that before. No, I do not claim it to be Earth."

"Less than thirty minutes ago, the temperature and atmosphere at any point down there would have made your existence in this form impossible."

"You don't say! I can only assure you that I am what I appear to be, gentlemen: an all too common variety of *Homo sapiens*. Either way, I am too ordinary, James. I am surprised you've always thought so highly of me. The errors, the unforgivable errors I made. McClellan at first appeared to me a veritable Napoleon; Grant seemed a whisky-befuddled barbarian . . ." He shook his head. "There were so many things I could have done to end the war earlier, to save so many lives, so much suffering . . ."

"I'm sure you did all you could—"

"Why do you stop, James? Afraid of showing compassion? It is the noblest of qualities . . . I am certain there is an answer to these contradictions you point up so well." His frown suddenly dissolved. "Yes, that's it, of course. You are both invited to disembark with me. You will receive the answers down there. There is no need to hurry your decision, Captain. I am most anxious to inspect a vessel which at least *appears* to float on air."

"We shall be honored," Kirk said. "Mr. Spock, inform the others. We'll consider this in the Briefing Room in one hour."

Lincoln looked around again. "Fascinating!" he said to Spock, smiling. "If I may borrow your favorite word."

"I'm flattered, sir."

"The smile lends attraction to your features, Mr. Spock."

Kirk turned, but Spock's face was as stony as always. "I'm afraid you're mistaken, sir," Kirk said. "Mr. Spock never smiles."

"Indeed?" Lincoln offered no further comment. Had he seen something behind Spock's expression? It would be in character.

They went up to the bridge, where the main viewing screen still showed a segment of the planet below them. Lincoln stared at it in awe, while Sulu and Chekov stared at him.

"Good Lord!"

"As I recall," Kirk said, "your Union Army observation balloons were tethered six hundred or so feet high, sir. We're six hundred forty-three miles above this planet."

"You can measure great distances that closely?"

"We do, sir," Spock said, moving to his station and checking his instruments. "Six hundred forty-three miles, two thousand twenty-one feet, two point zero four inches at this moment, in your old-style measurement."

"Bless me."

Uhura came onto the bridge. "Excuse me, Captain—"

"What a charming Negress," Lincoln said, then added quickly, "Oh, forgive me, my dear. I know that in my day some used that term as a description of property."

"Why should I object to the term, sir?" Uhura said, smiling. "In our century, we've learned not to fear words."

Kirk said, "May I present our communications officer, Lt. Uhura."

Lincoln shook hands with her, returning the smile. "The foolishness of my own century had me apologizing where no offense was given."

"Actually," she said, "I feel my color much lovelier and superior to yours and the Captain's."

"Superior? Then some of the old problems still exist?"

"No, sir," Kirk said. "It's just that we've learned to each be delighted in what we are. The Vulcans learned that centuries before we did."

"It's basic to the Vulcan philosophy, sir," Spock said. "How an infinite variety of things combine to make existence worthwhile."

"Yes, of course," Lincoln said. "The philosophy of 'nome'—meaning 'all.'" He paused, his frown returning. "Now, how did I know that? Just as I seem to know that on the planet's surface you will meet one of the greatest Vulcans in all the long history of your planet. My mind does not hold the name. But I know that he will be there."

"Excuse me, Captain," Uhura said, "but Mr. Scott is waiting for you in the Briefing Room."

"Oh, yes. Mr. President, with your permission I should like to make Lt. Uhura your guide at this point; I have a meeting."

"I would be delighted."

"Then we'll rejoin you shortly, sir. Mr. Sulu, the con is yours until Mr. Scott returns to the bridge."

In the Briefing Room, as Kirk and Spock entered, McCoy was saying to Spock: "Where the devil are they?"

"Perhaps looking up a plate of haggis in the galley? They've been everywhere else."

"Sorry, gentlemen," Kirk said, crossing to the table. "We were delayed."

"Jim, I'd be the last to advise you on your command image—"

"I doubt that, Bones, but continue."

"Do I have to lay it out for you? Practically the entire crew has seen you treating this imposter like the real thing—when he can't possibly be the real article, Captain!"

"Lincoln died three centuries ago and more, on a planet hundreds of light years away." Scott jerked a thumb over his shoulder.

"More in that direction, Engineer," Spock said, pointing down and to the left.

"The exact direction doesn't matter, you pointed-eared hobgoblin! You're the Science Officer," added McCoy, "why aren't you—well, doing whatever Science Officers do at a time like this?"

"I am, Doctor. I am observing the alien."

"At last. At least someone agrees with us he's an alien."

"Yes, he's an alien, of course," Kirk said after a moment's hesitation.

"And potentially dangerous," McCoy pressed on.

"Mad!" said Scott. "Loony as an Arcturian dog-bird."

"Spock and I have been invited to beam down to the planet's surface with him. Comments on that?"

"A big one," McCoy said. "Suddenly, miraculously, we see a small spot of Earth-type environment appear down there. Is it really there or do we just think we see it there?"

"You could beam down into a sea of molten lava," Scott said. "At the moment it's a raftlike mineral crust several hundred meters thick, over a molten iron core. It looks stable, but it was notably unstable in its formative phase."

"And there are transient images of life forms," McCoy said. "Minerallike themselves. Jim, that patch of Earth was created after our ship was scanned. Whoever they are, they examined us, determined our needs and supplied them down there. It smells, Captain. It's a trap."

"But why would they want to destroy only two of us?" Kirk said.

"It would be illogical of them, with such abilities," Spock said. "They could as easily trick us into destroying the entire vessel."

"Spock, are you implying that it's probably safe to beam down?"

"I am not, Doctor. There's no doubt that they want us down there for some hidden purpose. Otherwise they would have revealed some logical reason for all of this."

"Why Lincoln, Spock?" Kirk said. "Any speculation on that?"

"I need not speculate when the reason is obvious, Captain. President Lincoln has always been a very personal hero to you. What better way to titillate your curiosity than to make him come alive for you?"

"Not only to me, Spock."

"Agreed. I felt his charm, too. He is a magnificent work of duplication."

"But he has a *special* emotional involvement for you," McCoy said. "Interesting, since you're the one who will make the decision whether or not to beam down."

"Don't do it, Captain," Scott said.

Kirk thought about it. Finally he said, "The very reason for the existence of our starships is contact with other life. Although the method is beyond our comprehension, we *have* been offered contact. I'm beaming down. As for you, however, Mr. Spock—"

Spock stood. "Since I was included in their invitation to make contact, I must beam down with you, Captain."

McCoy exploded. "You're both out of your heads!"

"And you're on the edge of insubordination, Doctor," Kirk said.

"Would I be insubordinate to remind the Captain that this has the smell of things happening to him which I may not be able to patch back together this time?"

"Aye," Scott growled.

"Your concern noted and appreciated, gentlemen," Kirk said. "Mr. Spock, standard uniform, phasers and tricorder. Mr. Scott, have President Lincoln guided to the Transporter Room; we'll beam down immediately."

The three materialized in what seemed to be a wild canyon. The slopes were steep and boulder-strewn; on the floors there were shrubbery and trees. Kirk looked around.

"Captain!" Spock said. "Our weapons and tricorders did not beam down."

Kirk reached under his shirt and found his communicator still there, although his phaser and tricorder had indeed vanished. "Captain to *Enterprise*, come in . . . *Enterprise*, come in . . ."

Spock was also trying, but quickly gave over in favor of a careful examination of his communicator. "Undamaged," he reported. "Yet something prevents them from functioning."

Kirk swung angrily to Lincoln. "Your explanation, sir."

"I have none, Captain. To me this seems quite as it should be."

"Why have our weapons been taken? Why can't we communicate with our ship?"

"Please believe me. I know nothing other than what I have already told you—"

"The game's over! We've treated you with courtesy, we've gone along with who and what you think you are—"

"Despite the seeming contradictions, all is as it appears to be. I *am* Abraham Lincoln—"

"Just," another voice entered, "as I am who I appear to be."

Another man was approaching them: a tall, distinguished Vulcan. It was obvious that he was old, but as erect and strong as was usual with Vulcans even in age. The dignity and wisdom apparent in his features and bearing matched those of Lincoln's.

"Surak!" Spock said, in outright open astonishment.

"Who?" Kirk said.

"The greatest who ever lived on our planet, Captain. The father of all we became."

Surak stopped and made the Vulcan hand sign. "Live long and prosper, Spock. May you also, Captain Kirk."

"It is not logical that you are Surak," Spock said. "There is no fact, extrapolation from fact, or theory which would make it possible—"

"Whatever I am, Spock, would it harm you to give response?"

Spock slowly lifted his hand and returned the sign. "Live long and prosper, image of Surak, father of all we now hold true."

The newcomer almost smiled. "The image of Surak read in your face what was in your mind, Spock."

"As I turned and beheld you, I displayed emotion. I beg forgiveness."

Surak nodded gravely. "The cause was more than sufficient. We need speak no further of it. Captain, in my time, we knew not of Earthmen. And I am pleased to see we have differences. May we together become greater than the sum of both of us."

"Spock," Kirk said in an iron voice, "we will not go along with these charades any longer!"

He was answered by still another new voice, seemingly out of the air—an oddly reverberating voice. "You will have the answer soon, Captain."

A strange, shrilling sound, a little like the chiming of bells, followed the voice, and then, directly before the four, there was a rainbow flashing which congealed slowly into a bizarre shape. It was a creature made seemingly of rock, about the size and shape of a man but with clawlike appendages and a mouth which, like a cave, seemed to be permanently open. It was seated in a rock chair carved to fit its body.

"I am Yarnek," the voice reverberated from the open maw. "Our world is called Excalbia. Countless who live on that planet are watching. Before this drama unfolds, we give welcome to the ones named Kirk and Spock."

"We know nothing of your world or customs," Kirk said. "What do you mean by a drama about to unfold?"

"You are intelligent life forms. I am surprised you do not perceive the honor we do you." A claw gestured. "Have we not created in this place on our planet a stage identical to your own world?"

"We perceive only that we were invited down here and came in friendship. You have deprived us of our instruments for examining your world, of our means of defending ourselves and of communicating with our vessel."

"Your objection is well taken. We shall communicate with your vessel so that your fellow life forms may also enjoy and profit from the play. Behold . . . we begin."

At these words, four figures came into view at the edge of the glade, and approached cautiously. One was a squat human in a Mongol costume of about the 13th century; another, also human, in the uniform of a 21st century Colonel; one was a Klingon, and the last a female Tiburon. Except for the Colonel, who was dapper and not unhandsome, they were an ugly-looking lot.

"Some of these you may know through history," Yarnek said. "Genghis Khan, for one. And Colonel Green, who led a genocidal war in the 21st century on Earth. Kahless the Unforgettable, the Klingon who set the pattern for his planet's tyrannies. Zora, who experimented with the body chemistry of subject tribes on Tiburon.

"We welcome the vessel *Enterprise* to our solar system and our spectacle. We ask you to observe with us the confrontation of the two opposing philosophies you term 'good' and 'evil.' Since this is our first experiment with Earthlings, our theme is a simple one: survival. Life and death. Your philosophies are alien to us, and we wish to understand them and discover which is the stronger. We learn by observing such spectacles."

"What do you mean, survival?" Kirk said.

"The word is explicit. If you and Spock survive, you may return to your vessel. If you do not, your existence is ended. Your choice of action is unlimited, as is your choice of weapons, should you wish to use any—you may fabricate anything you desire out of what you find around you. Let the spectacle begin."

"Mr. Spock and I refuse to participate."

"You will decide otherwise," Yarnek said, and then dissolved into that same mist of rainbows from which he had emerged.

"Analysis, Spock. Why do they want us to fight?"

"It may be exactly as explained, Captain. Our concept of good and evil would be strange to them. They wish to see which is strongest."

"And they'll have the answer if it kills us. Do you recall the exact location where we beamed down?"

"We have strayed from it somewhat, Captain. It was in that area, beyond those boulders."

"Ship's coordinates may still be locked in there." He started toward the spot, ignoring the others, Spock following. Lincoln and Surak were soon lost from view; but after a moment, rounding a large boulder, Kirk found himself face to face with them again. After staring at them, Kirk tried again, taking another path—with the same result.

"Mr. Spock?"

"I have no explanation, sir. Unless the creature is compelling us to circle. Quite obviously it is preventing us from reaching that area."

"I'm afraid, Captain," Lincoln said, "that none of us may leave until we do what it demands of us."

From the group of potentional antagonists, Colonel Green stepped forward, his hand extended in a gesture of peace. His manner seemed friendly, even intended to charm. "Captain Kirk. May I? I'm Colonel Green. I quite agree with your attitude toward this charade. It's ridiculous to expect us to take part in it."

Kirk looked at him with open suspicion, and Green stopped while he was still a few steps away. "What do you want?"

"Exactly what you do. To get out of here. I have no quarrel with you, any more than you have with me."

"You're somewhat different from the way history paints you, Colonel."

"History tends to exaggerate," Green said with a small laugh. "I suggest we call a halt to this at once, and see if we can't find a way out of our difficulties. My associates are in full agreement with me."

Kirk looked beyond him at the "associates." Zora bowed gravely. Khan was hunkered down on the ground; apparently he was bored. Well, he had never been much of a man for talk. Kahless looked around curiously at the slopes.

"You were tricked into coming here, weren't you?" Green said. "So were we all."

"Where did you come from?"

"I don't remember . . . Isn't that strange? My memory used to be quite remarkable." He came closer, took Kirk's elbow confidentially, drawing him to one side. "But wherever it was, I want to get back. So it seems to me, Captain, that we have common cause, and that our enemy is that creature."

"What do you propose?"

"That we combine forces and reason out some way to overcome it. Are we in agreement?"

Kirk hesitated, studying him. "As I recall, Colonel, you were notorious for striking out at your enemies in the midst of negotiating with them."

"But that was centuries ago, Captain!" Green said, with a louder laugh. "And not altogether true! There is much that I'd change now if I could. Don't let prejudice and rumor sway you."

"Captain!" Spock shouted.

Suddenly everything seemed to be happening at once. Swinging, Kirk saw in a flash that Khan had somehow gotten to higher ground and was holding a boulder over his head in both hands. Then Green's arm was locked around Kirk's neck and he was thrown halfway to the ground. Kirk lashed out, staggering Green, and as he sprang to his feet saw Lincoln wrestling with Khan, who seemed to have missed whomever he had been aiming the boulder at.

Then the brawl was over as suddenly as it had begun, the four antagonists vanished among the boulders and trees of the canyon. Total silence swept over them. Breathing hard, Kirk joined the other three. All had been battered, Spock severely.

"Is anyone hurt?" Kirk said.

"I fear my clothing is somewhat damaged," Lincoln said. "But how delightful to discover at my age that I can still wrestle."

"Mr. Spock?"

"Quite all right, Captain. However, I suggest that we prepare ourselves for another attack."

"No," Kirk said. "Green was right. That rocklike thing, Yarnek, is the enemy. Not those illusions."

"For an illusion, my opponent had a remarkable grip," Lincoln said, "But I forgot. You consider me an illusion, too."

"The Captain speaks wisely," Surak said. "These four are not our enemy. We should arrive together at a peaceful settlement."

The bell-like trilling began once more, and with it the rainbow swirling. Yarnek was back.

"I am disappointed," the creature said. "You display no interest in the honor we do you. We offer you an opportunity to become our teachers. By demonstrating whether good or evil is more powerful—"

Kirk lunged at the creature. It did not move—but when Kirk seized it, it was as though he had tried to grab a red-hot stove. With a yell he snatched his hands back.

"You find my body heat distressing?" Yarnek said.

"You forget the nature of this planet ... I must conclude that your species requires a cause to fight for. You may now communicate with your ship."

Kirk fumbled for his communicator, and despite the pain of his seared hands, managed to flip it open. "Kirk to *Enterprise*. Come in. Kirk to *Enterprise*, Do you read me?"

"Be patient, Captain," Yarnek said. "They read you."

Suddenly the communicator came alive in a bedlam of shouting voices, backed up by the sound of the ship's alarm. The bridge was obviously in turmoil.

"Mr. Scott!" Uhura called. "The Captain is trying to reach us."

"Engineering!" Scout was shouting. "Give me that again, man, I canna hear you."

"Deterioration has just started, sir."

"What is it, Lieutenant?" Kirk demanded.

"Where?" Scott shouted.

"Red Alert, Captain," Uhura said. "Mr. Scott is standing by."

"In the shielding between matter and antimatter. I don't know what started it."

"What caused the alert?"

"I don't know, sir. Mr. Scott, I have the Captain."

"Check for radiation. Get a repair crew on it at once."

"I have already, sir. We can't seem to stop it."

"Is there danger of detonation?"

"Estimate four hours, sir."

"Mr. Scott, sir, I have the Captain!"

"What? Oh—Captain, Scott here."

"Beam us aboard fast, Scotty."

"I canna, sir. There's a complete power failure. We're on emergency battery power only."

"What's happening?"

"I can't explain it, sir. Matter and antimatter are in Red Zone proximity. No knowing how it started and no stopping it either. The shielding is breaking down. Estimate four hours before it goes completely. That'll blow us up for fair!"

"The estimate is quite correct," Yarnek's hollow voice said. "Your ship will blow itself to atoms within four hours, Captain—unless you defeat the others before then. Is that cause enough to fight for?"

"What if they defeat us?"

"To save your ship and your crew, you have to win."

"Scotty, alert Starfleet Command. Disengage nacelles and jettison if possible. Scotty, do you read me?"

"Your communicators once more no longer function," Yarnek said. "You may proceed with the spectacle." With a chime and a shimmer, the creature was gone.

"The war is forced upon us, Captain," Lincoln said. "History repeats itself."

"Well," Kirk said, "I see nothing immoral in fighting illusions. It's play their game, fight, or lose the ship and every crewman aboard."

Spock looked toward Surak. "And if they're real, Captain?"

Kirk chose to let that go by. "We'll use the top of the defile as a base. It's defensible. They can't approach without our seeing them."

"Are we fighting a defensive war, James?" Lincoln said.

"We don't have the time. But if it goes against us I want a place to retreat to. Right now I want to scout them out, find their weaknesses and attack."

Lincoln smiled. "Do you drink whisky?"

"Occasionally," Kirk said, startled. "Why?"

"Because you have qualities very much like those of another man I admired greatly. One I mentioned before—General Grant."

The reminder of the possible illusory nature of all this was jarring, distracting. "Thank you. We'll need weapons. Spock, I believe the primitive Vulcans made something like a boomerang."

"Yes, Captain. However—"

"Spears, too. Slings. Mr. President, you used slings as a boy—"

"Indeed I did." Lincoln stripped off his coat, pulled

out his shirttail and ripped from it a long strip. Again that conflict of realism and illusion.

"Captain," Spock said, "logic dictates that we consider another course." He looked deferentially toward Surak, who thus far had remained a profoundly troubled nonparticipant in the discussion.

"In my time on Vulcan we too faced these alternatives," Surak said. "We had suffered devastating wars that nearly destroyed our planet and another was about to begin. We were torn. And out of our suffering some of us found the discipline to act. We sent emissaries to our opponents to propose peace. The first were killed. Others followed. Ultimately, we achieved peace, which has lasted since then."

"The circumstances were different, Surak."

"The face of war never changes. Look at us, Captain. We have been hurt. So have they. Surely it is more logical to heal than kill."

"I'm afraid that kind of logic doesn't apply here," Kirk said.

"That is precisely why we should not fight—"

"*My ship is at stake!*"

Surak said, "I will not harm others, Captain."

"Sir," Spock said, "his convictions are most profound on this matter—"

"So are mine, Spock! If I believed there was a peaceful way out of this—"

"The risk would be mine alone, Captain," Surak said. "And if I fail, you would lose nothing. I am no warrior."

There was a moment of silence, while Kirk looked from one Vulcan to the other.

"The Captain knows that I have fought at his side before," Spock said. "And I will now if need be. But I too am Vulcan, bred to peace. Let us attempt it."

"You saw how treacherously they acted," Kirk said.

"Yes, Captain," Surak said. "But perhaps it is our belief in peace which is actually being tested."

"Wellll . . . I have no authority over you. Do as you think best."

"Thank you. May you live long and prosper." Surak

gave the Vulcan sign and went off. Kirk watched him depart, doubtful, but also with some awe. Then he shook the mood off.

"The weapons, gentlemen—in case he fails."

Time went past. The three fashioned crude spears, bolos, slings, boomerangs, and gathered rocks for throwing. Spock was visibly on edge; he kept looking after the vanished Surak.

"A brave man," Kirk said.

"Men of peace usually are, sir. On Vulcan he is revered as the Father of Civilization. The father-image has much meaning for us."

"You show emotion, Mr. Spock," Kirk said, and then was instantly sorry he had said it; this was surely no time for needling. But Spock replied only:

"I deeply respect what he accomplished."

"Let's hope he accomplishes something here."

As if on cue, the air was rent by a harrowing scream of agony.

"Surak!" Spock cried.

"Yes," Kirk said grimly. "I would guess that they're torturing him."

"Mr. Spock!" Colonel Green's voice called, from no very great distance off. "Your friend wants you. He seems to be hurt."

"Help me, Spock!" Surak's voice called, raw with pain.

"You can't let him suffer," Green said.

"Sir," Spock said, his face like stone. "They are trying to goad us into attacking rashly."

"I know that."

"And he was aware that this might happen when he went—" Spock was interrupted by another scream.

"I should not have let him go," Kirk said.

"You had no choice, Captain—" Another scream. It cut Kirk like a knife, but Spock went on through it. "You could not have stopped him."

"How can you ignore it?"

"I suspect it, sir. A Vulcan would not cry out so."

"So his suffering doesn't matter?"

"I am not insensitive to it, sir, nor am I ignoring it."

"I don't care whether he is Vulcan or not. He is in agony."

"The fact that he might not be Vulcan does not blind me to the fact."

The cry came again. "But you can listen to that and chop logic about it?" Kirk said. "Well, I can't!"

Kirk strode off toward the antagonists' camp. Spock was after him in one bound, grasping his arm.

"Captain, that is what they want of us. They are waiting for us to attempt a rescue."

"Perhaps we can rescue him, Mr. Spock," Lincoln said. "I suggest that we do exactly what they want."

"Do what they want?"

"Not the way they want it, however. We must first convince them that they have provoked us to recklessness. James? You seem taken aback. I do not mean to presume upon your authority—"

"It isn't that."

"What I propose to do is that I circle around to their rear while you two provide a frontal distraction. It should be sufficiently violent to cover what I do."

"Which is—?"

"Slip into their camp and free him."

"No," Kirk said.

"I was something of a backwoodsman, James. I doubt that you could do what I was bred to."

"I won't have you risk it."

"I am no longer President," Lincoln said, with a slight smile. "Mr. Spock, any comment?"

"No, sir."

"Then," Lincoln said, "one matter further, gentlemen. We fight on their level. With trickery, brutality, finality. We match their evil . . . You forget, James. I know I am reputed a gentle man. Kindly, I believe the word is. But I was Commander in Chief during the four bloodiest years of my country's history. I gave orders that sent a hundred thousand men to death by the hands of their brothers. There is no honorable way to kill, no gentle way to destroy. There is nothing good in war—except its ending. And you are fighting for the lives of your crew."

"Mr. President," Kirk said, "your campaign."

The scream came again. It was markedly weaker.

Khan and Green were on watch as Kirk and Spock worked their way among the boulders to the enemy camp. Kirk made no particular effort at concealment, "accidentally" showing himself several times. By the time they were in range, Zora and Kahless had appeared, weapons at the ready.

Kirk and Spock rose as one, threw spears, and ducked again. One of the spears narrowly missed Khan, who with a wild yell retaliated with a boulder that came equally close.

When Kirk looked again, Green was gone, and a moment later, so were Kahless and Zora. Then Green came back. What did that maneuver mean? But Kirk was left no time to see more; Green threw a spear at him with murderous accuracy, and he was forced to duck again.

Lincoln, creeping up at the rear, almost tripped a man-trap made of a tied-down sapling. Backing off, he deliberately tripped it, and then resumed crawling.

Ahead he could see Surak, bound to a tree, head slumped. No one else seemed to be around.

"Surak!" he called in a low voice. "I will have you free in a minute." Racing forward, he began to cut the thongs binding the Vulcan. "The others have drawn them away. We will circle around. It was a worthy effort, Surak. No need to blame yourself for its failure."

The thongs parted. As Lincoln put out a hand to help Surak, the Vulcan collapsed at his feet. He was dead.

"Help me, Lincoln!"

Lincoln spun. The voice had been Surak's, but it was coming from Kahless. He and Green were standing in the direction from which Lincoln had just come, grinning, spears ready.

It was only afterward that Kirk was able to sort the battle out. Their four antagonists had charged them, leaping with spears raised. Hit by a rock, Kirk stumbled and fell, and Zora was upon him at once; but whatever expertise she may have had in body chemistry, she was no fighter. Kirk rolled and threw her aside, hard. She was hurt and lay watching him in terror.

Nearby, Spock and Khan were fighting hand to hand. They seemed to be evenly matched, but Kirk had no chance to help—Kahless was upon him. The struggle was a violent, kaleidoscopic, head-banging eternity. When it stopped, very suddenly, it took Kirk several seconds to realize that he had killed the Klingon. Snatching up a spear, he ran at Khan, who broke free of Spock and fled, looking wildly behind him. Green was running now, too. Kirk snatched up a spear and threw it. He did not miss.

Then it was all over. Inside the enemy camp, they found the bodies of Lincoln and of Surak. They looked down with rage and grief. Neither could find anything to say.

Then, once more, the bell-like chiming sounded, and the seated, stony figure of Yarnek emerged from its cocoon of rainbows.

"You are the survivors," the echoing voice said. "The others have run off. It would appear that evil retreats when forcibly confronted. However, you have failed to demonstrate to me any other difference between your philosophies. Your good and your evil use the same methods, achieve the same results. Do you have an explanation?"

"You established the methods and the goals," Kirk said.

"For you to use as you chose."

"What did you offer them if they won?"

"What they wanted most—power."

"You offered me the lives of my crew."

"I perceive," Yarnak said. "You have won their lives."

Kirk boiled over. "How many others have you done

this to? What gives you the right to hand out life and death?"

"The same right that brought you here: the need to know new things."

"We came in peace—"

"And you may go in peace." Yarnak faded from view.

Kirk took out his communicator. "Kirk to *Enterprise* . . . Mr. Sulu, beam us aboard."

On the bridge everything seemed to be functioning normally, as though nothing had ever gone wrong.

"Mr. Spock," Kirk said. "Explanation?"

"Conjecture, sir, rather than explanation."

"Well?"

"It would seem that we were held in the power of creatures able to control matter, to rearrange molecules in whatever fashion they desired. So Yarnak was able to create the images of Surak and Lincoln and the others, after scanning our minds, by making use of its fellow creatures as source matter."

"They seemed so real, Spock. To me, especially, Mr. Lincoln. I feel I actually met Lincoln."

Spock nodded. "And Surak. In a sense, perhaps they were, Captain. Created out of our own thoughts, how could they be anything but what we expected them to be?"

"It was so hard to see him die once again. I begin to understand what Earth endured to achieve final peace." Kirk paused. "Mr. Spock . . . is there a memorial to Surak on Vulcan?"

"Yes, sir. A monument of great beauty. However, it is held generally that the true memorial to him is the peace and the friendship that have endured among Vulcans since his time with them."

"The same with Lincoln. I think of all our heroes on Earth, he is the most loved today. We see his dreams around us. We have the brotherhood and equality of men that he hoped for, and we're still learning what he knew instinctively."

"Men of such stature live beyond their years."

"They were alive today, Spock. Those were more than rearranged molecules we saw."

"We projected into them our own concepts of them, sir."

"Did we?" After a moment, Kirk shook his head. "There is still much of their work to be done in the galaxy, Spock ... Mr. Sulu, break orbit for our next assignment."

THE LIGHTS OF ZETAR
(Jeremy Tarcher and Shari Lewis)

The *Enterprise* was enroute to Memory Alpha when the storm first appeared. Memory Alpha was a planetoid set up by the Federation solely as a central library containing the total cultural history and scientific knowledge of all planetary Federation members. The ship had a passenger, Lt. Mira Romaine, an attractive woman of about thirty. She was on board to supervise the transfer of newly designed equipment which the *Enterprise* was also carrying. At the moment, she was on the bridge talking to Scott at his position.

"Mr. Scott, I hope I haven't been too much trouble to you with all the questions I've asked."

"Well, I'm sorry the trip is coming to an end," Scott said. "I'm going to miss your questions."

Kirk watched them amusedly. "Present position, Mr. Chekov?"

"On course—one seventy-two mark four."

"Mr. Scott, as soon as we are within viewing range of Memory Alpha, you and Lt. Romaine will go to your stations in the emergency manual monitor. Prepare for direct transfer of equipment."

"Yes, Captain."

"We're ready, sir," Mira added.

"Lieutenant," Spock said, "may I offer my congratulations on what will be a first in the Federation."

"And good luck," Kirk added.

"Thank you, Mr. Spock, Captain."

"I didn't think Mr. Scott would go for the brainy type," Chekov said, almost too softly for Kirk to overhear.

"I don't think he's even noticed she has a brain. Has she?" Sulu said. A red light came up on his panel. "Captain, I am picking up a high intensity reading. Shall I display it?"

"Yes." Kirk looked at the main viewing screen. In the blackness of space there was a faint light source. "Is that Memory Alpha?"

"No, sir."

"Magnification eight."

The light now showed as a cloud of vaguely organic shape, almost like a brain. It sparked and flashed intermittently in varied hues, like a series of inspired thoughts.

"Is that some kind of storm?" Kirk said.

"Quite possible, Captain," Spock said. "I've never seen one of such great intensity and strange conformation."

"Captain," Sulu added, "it is approaching at warp two point six and accelerating."

"Recheck your readings, Mr. Sulu. It is impossible for a natural phenomenon to move faster than the speed of light."

"It is definitely doing so," Spock confirmed—and indeed the thing was visibly growing on the screen. "It therefore cannot be a phenomenon of nature."

"Deflector on. Condition yellow."

The light source filled the screen. The glare was almost unbearable. Then the screen went blank.

Kirk tried to snap out an order and found that he could not. The whole bridge was suddenly deathly silent. No one moved.

Then, just as abruptly, it was over. "Mr. Sulu, full scan on that turbulence or whatever it was!" Kirk noticed Scott staring uncertainly over Kirk's own shoulder. Turning to see what he was looking at, he was just in time to see Mira crumple out of sight behind the command chair.

"Mira!" Scott leapt from his post, knelt beside her and lifted her head off the floor. "Mira!"

She murmured unintelligibly. It was not that the sounds were indistinct, but as though they were in an unknown language.

"What's that you're saying?" Scott said. Kirk and Spock were now also bending close. The strange murmuring went on.

McCoy came onto the bridge and crossed at once to the group, his tricorder already out and in use. He said, "Was she hurt by the fall or by the action of that . . . disturbance?"

"I don't know," Kirk said. "You were closest, Scotty. Did you notice?"

"She collapsed when it was over."

McCoy gave her a shot. The murmuring died away. Her expression changed from a curiously rapt look to one of relaxation. Then her eyes opened and she looked around in confusion.

"Easy now," Scott said. "You took quite a fall."

"I'm fine now," she said.

"Let me be the judge," McCoy said. "Can you walk to Sickbay?"

"Doctor, I'm fine, really I am." Again she looked around the bridge, obviously still puzzled. "Is everyone else—all right?"

"Aye, they are," Scott said. "You do just as Dr. McCoy says."

"Why? I never felt better in my—"

"Lieutenant, report to Sickbay," Kirk said. "That's an order."

"Yes, sir." She followed McCoy resignedly toward the elevator.

Scott said, "Would it be all right for me to go to Sickbay?"

"You will stay at your post, Mr. Scott. Lt. Uhura, damage report, all stations."

"All stations are operative."

"Mr. Spock?"

"Some equipment was temporarily out of order. My sensors were inoperative."

"Any damage to the warp engines?"

"None, Captain."

"Good. From the action of that—that storm, we may need all the speed we can get."

"It was not a storm, Captain," Spock said.

"Mr. Chekov, get a fix on whatever it was and try to project its path . . . That was a novel experience for the *Enterprise*. Would you agree, Mr. Spock?"

"Unforgettable, Captain."

"Yes? I was hoping you had an explanation."

"None at the moment, Captain. Only a sharply etched memory of what I felt during the onslaught."

"Memory Alpha was hailing us a moment before," Uhura said. "I wanted to respond, but I couldn't make my hand move."

"It was not hands that were paralyzed, it was eyes," Chekov said. "I couldn't force my eyes to look down to set a new course."

"No," Sulu said, "speech was affected. I couldn't utter a sound."

"Nor could I," Kirk said. "You seemed to be having the same trouble, Mr. Spock."

"Yes, Captain, I was."

"Any explanation yet?"

"Only of the result," Spock said, "none of the cause. In each case, different areas of the brain were affected. Our voluntary nerve functions were under some form of pressure."

"Or of attack?"

"Attack might be a more precise formulation, Captain."

"Lt. Romaine seems most susceptible. Mr. Scott, perhaps you'd better go down to Sickbay after all. If she was the only one of four hundred and thirty people who passed out, we'd better find out why."

"Aye, sir," Scott said, heading for the elevators with alacrity.

"I have plotted the storm's path, Captain," Chekov

said. "On its present course it will hit the Memory Alpha planetoid as it did us."

"Uhura, warn them of the proximity of the phenomenon. Can you give us an ETA for it, Chekov?"

"It's impossible, Captain. It has the ability to change speed."

"Sorry, Captain," Uhura said, "But I'm unable to establish contact with the planetoid. Am hailing on all frequencies. No response."

"It does not matter, Captain," Spock said. "Memory Alpha has no protective shields. When the library complex was assembled, shielding was regarded as inappropriate to its totally academic purpose. Since the information on the memory planet is freely available to everyone, special protection was deemed unnecessary."

"Wonderful," Kirk said sarcastically. "I hope the 'storm' is aware of that rationale."

"We're completing approach to the planetoid," Sulu said. "But the storm's gotten there first."

"Uhura, get through to—"

"I cannot," Uhura said. "I cannot get past the interference, sir."

"Mr. Spock, how many people are there on Memory Alpha?"

"It varies with the number of scholars, researchers, scientists, from various Federation planets who are using the computer complex."

"Mr. Chekov, maintain standard orbit."

"The storm is now leaving Memory Alpha," Sulu reported.

"And," Spock added, "the sensors give no readings of energy being generated on the planetoid."

"Any life readings?"

"None, sir."

"Check for malfunction."

Spock did so. "Sensors inoperative again."

"We'd better find out what's going on down there." Kirk turned to the intercom. "Kirk to Sickbay. Is Mr. Scott there?"

"Scott here. I was checking on the lass. She's going to be fine, though. Nothing wrong with her."

"I'm relieved to hear your prognosis. Is the doctor there with you?"

"McCoy here, Jim."

"How's the girl?"

"I think she's in good shape."

"Apparently Scotty thinks so, too. Both of you, meet me in the Transporter Room, on the double. Mr. Spock, come with me. The con is yours, Mr. Sulu."

The four materialized in a computer room on Memory Alpha. The room was utterly silent, and there was no light at all.

"Somehow," McCoy grumbled, "I find transporting into the darkness unnerving."

"Scotty," Kirk said, "can you give us some light in here?"

Scott checked the boards nearby; they could hear him fumbling. Then a small glow appeared, a safe-light of some sort. "This will have to do. The generator is inoperative. The alternative is to go back to the ship for hand torches."

Spock moved to the face of the largest computer cabinet with his tricorder, but for several moments simply stood there, doing nothing. Kirk guessed he was waiting for his eyes to become dark-adapted, a gift far better developed in Vulcans than in humans. Then he lifted the tricorder.

"Damage report, Mr. Spock?"

"It's a disaster for the galaxy, Captain. The central brain damaged—all memory cores burned out. The loss might be irretrievable."

Kirk took a step and stumbled over something large and soft. He put a hand down to it, but he too could see better now.

"Mr. Spock. I've just encountered a body. Look around the floor."

There was a long silence. Then Spock said: "There are dead men and creatures from other planets sprawled all around us. Move very carefully until you can see better. I'm scanning for a life reading . . . Yes, I have one, very faint."

"Location, Mr. Spock?"

"It is too weak to get an exact bearing, but . . ." He moved away.

"We'd better find him while he's still alive. We have to get more knowledge of this . . . enemy."

"Over here, Captain," Spock's voice called.

The other three carefully moved toward the sound of his voice. At his feet a girl, evidently a technician, was on her knees, struggling to get up. An already dead man nearby had evidently tried to help her. She was murmuring.

Spock listened intently. "The same garbled sounds," he said, "that Lt. Romaine was making when she fainted after the disturbance."

"Are you sure, Spock?"

"Absolutely sure."

Kirk flipped open his communicator. "Kirk to *Enterprise* . . . Mr. Sulu. Beam down Lt. Romaine immediately—and have her bring five hand torches."

"Yes, sir."

The technician's voice murmured on, but it was becoming steadily weaker. Then she pitched forward on her face.

McCoy took a reading, and then silently shook his head. Kirk said: "Can you tell what she died of?"

"Severe brain hemorrhaging due to distortion of all neural centers. Dissolution of all basic personality patterns. Even the autonomic nervous system."

"The attack, Captain, was thorough," Spock said.

"What did the others die of?"

"Each had a different brain center destroyed," McCoy said. "Just how, I can't tell you. Maybe when I get back to the ship's computer—"

The shimmer of the Transporter effect briefly illumated the charnel chamber and Mira materialized. The beam of a flashlight leapt from her hand, but Scott moved swiftly to step into it, blocking her view of the bodies.

"Mira—the Captain has some questions. Give me the rest of the torches."

"Here you are . . . Yes, Captain?"

Kirk said gently: "Mira, while you were unconscious you were, uh, speaking."

"What did I say?" She seemed genuinely surprised.

"We don't know. You talked in a strange language we didn't understand. We found one person barely alive in here, and she was speaking in the same way—"

"Was speaking?" Before anyone could move to prevent her, she darted around the central computer and swept the beam of her flash over the floor. When she spoke again, it was in a frightened whisper. "All dead . . . just like I saw them. Captain, we must get back to the ship."

"Why?"

Her hands went to her brow. She seemed unable to answer.

"Tell me why!"

"Captain—that . . . that . . . it's returning!"

"How do you know?"

"I know. You'll be killed if we stay."

"I assure you, lieutenant," Spock said, "that unexplained phenomenon was headed away from the planetoid before we came here. It is probably seeking other victims."

"I tell you, it will kill us!" Her panic was genuine, that was clear.

Kirk's communicator beeped. "Bridge to Captain Kirk. The storm has reappeared on the long-range scanner."

"I told him it is not a storm," Spock said.

"Course, Mr. Sulu?"

"Coming back in this direction, and closing fast."

"Beam us up."

The minute he saw the Transporter Room coming into being around him, Kirk headed for the intercom, but Scott's voice stopped him.

"Captain, wait! We've lost Mira."

Kirk turned and saw that Lt. Romaine was indeed

not there. Lt. Kyle was at the Transporter controls. Scott leaped to his side.

"Where is she? Stabilize her!"

"Something's interfering with the transporter signal," Kyle said. "I have her coordinates, but she's suspended in transit."

"Let me." Together the two men struggled with the controls. Suddenly, Kyle said, "Aha, it's cleared," and at the same moment Mira materialized on the Transporter platform. She stepped off, dazed but smiling.

"Mr. Scott, Lt. Romaine, you'd best go to the emergency manual monitor and see if enough new equipment is in inventory to repair at least some of Memory Alpha." Kirk hit the intercom. "Mr. Sulu, get us out of here. Mr. Spock, to the bridge, please."

In the emergency manual monitor, Mira and Scott were working side by side. The inventory had proceeded for some time in silence. Then Scott said:

"When I—thought we lost you, back there in the Transporter Room—well, you're not to do that again."

"It was so frightening," she said. "I felt pulled apart."

"You almost were. There was interference with the Transporter mechanism."

"And that's more than you can say about me," she said. What she meant by this, Scott had no idea.

"I'll tell you something. You are the sanest—the smartest—the nicest—and the most beautiful woman that has ever been aboard this ship."

"And what else?"

"Anything else, I'm keeping to myself for the moment."

"But I'm so much trouble to you."

"Trouble? What trouble? Of course, you could drive a man daft, but that's not what I call trouble."

She smiled. "Do I drive you daft, Scotty?"

"Well now—if it was me, you might have to work at it."

"I'd be willing—" Then, as if embarrassed, she turned away and resumed being busy.

"The *Enterprise* has been my life," Scott said. "I love this ship, and I love every day I've spent on it. But, until you came aboard, I didn't know how lonely it is to be free in the galaxy . . . So, don't you talk of trouble." He took her in his arms. "Now I want to forget about Memory Alpha."

It was the wrong thing to say. She pushed against his chest, her hands trembling. "Scotty . . . before that . . . I saw it—exactly as it happened."

"What of it? That happens to lots of people. There's a French term for it. They think they're seeing something before it actually occurs. But actually one eye picked it up without realizing—"

"My eyes weren't playing tricks!"

He smoothed her brow. "Then I'm sure there is some other perfectly reasonable explanation that will erase that worried frown."

"But Scotty, I saw the men dead in their exact positions—before I ever left the ship."

He put his hands on her shoulders. "Listen to me. I told you in Sickbay what strange tricks a first trip in space can play on your mind. That's all it is."

"No, Scotty."

"Have you ever had visions of future events before this?"

"Never."

"And, if you ask me, *nobody* ever has," Scott said firmly. "That seeing the future is pure bunk. You know that, don't you?"

"I always believed it."

"And you're absolutely right."

"But what is it, Scotty? What is frightening me? Ever since we've been near that—that storm, I've had such strange thoughts . . . feelings of such terror."

"Space, space, space, that's all it is."

"Then I don't have to report it?"

"If you want to spend the trip in Sickbay," Scott said. "But what good would it do? McCoy can no more cure it than he can cure a cold. It'll pass."

"When I get my permanent assignment . . . I hope it will be to the *Enterprise*."

"You just better make sure of it."

"Captain," Sulu said. "It's changing course."

"Plot it, Mr. Chekov."

"Present course will bring it across our starboard bow."

"Mr. Spock, you made a statement that that phenomenon was not a storm."

"Yes, Captain. No known conditions in space would support it as a natural phenomenon. But the sensors seem to be in working order at the moment. Perhaps this time the elusive creature will reveal something about itself." He bent into his hooded viewer. "It seems to be maintaining its distance, but matching course with us. I am receiving increasing magnitudes of energy. Yes—undoubtedly a life form. Fascinating!"

"Control your fascination, Mr. Spock. Pragmatically, what are the implications?"

"We saw the results of full contact in the deaths on Memory Alpha. The humanoid neurological system is destroyed when fully exposed to these peculiar wave patterns."

"But what *is* it, Spock?"

"Not what is it, sir. What are they. There are ten distinct life units within it, Captain. They are powerfully alive and vital."

"Who are they? Where are they from?"

"Impossible to determine without programming for computer analysis."

"Not now." Kirk shot a glance at the main viewer. "It's clear we can't outrun them. Can we shield against them?"

"I do not think so, sir."

"There must be some defensive action we can take."

"Captain, it is a community of life units. Their attack is in the form of brain waves directed against the brain that is most compatible."

"A living brain!" Kirk said. "Perhaps we can avoid a

next time. Lt. Uhura, open all channels and tie in the universal translator. Maybe I can talk to them."

Uhura got to work. Indicators began to light up. "All channels open," she said finally. "Translator tied in."

Kirk looked up at the form of lights on the viewer. Incongruously, he felt wryly amused at the notion of trying to talk to an electrical cloud. "This is Captain James Kirk of the USS *Enterprise*. We wish you no harm. Physical contact between us is fatal to our life form. Please do not come any closer to this ship."

There was no response; only a faint wash of static. Spock said, "Perhaps it did not understand."

"Captain, change in velocity recorded," Sulu said. "It has accelerated its approach."

"Perhaps it will understand another language," Kirk said, beginning to feel angry. "Condition Red Alert. Prepare for phaser firing."

The Red Alert began flashing, and the distant alarm echoed throughout the ship.

"Mr. Sulu, lock in phasers for firing across their course. Do not hit them."

"Locked in, sir."

"Fire."

The phaser shot lanced to one side of the lights and on off into deep space.

"Reaction, Mr. Sulu?"

"None, sir. They are still approaching."

Apparently a shot across the bow was insufficiently convincing. "Lock to target."

"Locked on, sir."

"Fire."

The shot seemed to score a direct hit. The community of life units dispersed in apparent confusion, and then began to reform. So they *could* be hurt—

"Captain, Captain," Scott's voice shouted from the intercom, without even waiting for an acknowledgment. "Scott here. The phaser shots—they're killing Mira."

"Killing Lt. Romaine? How—"

"When you fired, she was stunned, she crumpled. Another shot and you'll kill her."

"Get her to Sickbay at once . . . Mr. Spock, we appear to be at an impasse. Any suggestions?"

"Only one, Captain," the Science Officer said. "There seems to be only one possible defense. If we can find an environment that is deadly to the life form—and at the same time, isolate the girl from the deadly effects of it—"

"It sounds like asking the impossible." Kirk turned to the intercom. "Kirk to Dr. McCoy . . . Bones, is Lt. Romaine well enough to be talked to?"

"I think so," McCoy's voice said. "I can have her ready in a few minutes."

"Bring her and Mr. Scott to the Briefing Room as soon as possible. Bring all available biographical data on the lieutenant. . . . Mr. Spock, come with me."

In the Briefing Room, Spock went immediately to his slave console; Kirk sat at the center of the table, McCoy next to him.

"Go easy on her, Jim. She's in a bad state."

"I'll try. But this can't be postponed."

"I know. I was pretty hard on her myself the first time this happened. I needn't have been. We might know more."

"I'll be careful."

The door opened to admit Scott and Mira. He was holding her by the arm. She seemed pale and distraught. After she was seated, Scott went to his chair at the opposite end of the table.

Kirk leaned toward her and said gently: "This is not a trial, Lt. Romaine. You are not being accused of anything."

"I know," Mira said, almost in a whisper. She glanced toward McCoy. "I didn't mean to be uncooperative, Doctor."

"Of course you didn't," McCoy said. "I told the Captain that."

"I'll tell you everything I know. I trust all of you implicitly. I want to help."

"Good," Kirk said. "This investigation is prompted by two events that may be connected. The first time was when you passed out on the bridge. The second is when we fired the ship's phasers into the force that is attacking us, and we seriously injured you."

"It wasn't serious, Captain. You mustn't worry about hurting me."

"We're glad we didn't. Nevertheless, we won't take that particular defense measure again. Now, this is how we will proceed. Spock will provide everything we know about our attackers. Dr. McCoy has access to Starfleet's exhaustive file on you. A comparison of the two may turn up some unsuspected connection that will protect you—and ourselves. All right, gentlemen? Dr. McCoy, you begin. Does Lt. Romaine have any history of psychosomatic illness?"

"Occasional and routine teen-age incidence."

"Any evidence of any involuntary or unconscious telepathatic abilities?"

"None."

"Any pathological or unusual empathic responses?"

"No, Captain. Not empathic. However, an exceptionally flexible and pliant response to new learning situations."

At this Spock leaned forward, but made no comment.

"There's one other thing, Captain," McCoy said. "Right after our phasers hit that thing, I gave Lt. Romaine the Steinman Standard Analysis. I don't have the results here but Nurse Chapel is having it sent down. In the meantime, I see nothing else very illuminating in the psychological file. Lt. Romaine has developed strong defenses to guard against her extreme competitiveness. Marked scientific and mathematical abilities set up an early competition with her distinguished father. It appears that the problem is still not completely resolved."

"That's not true," Mira said, tears coming to her eyes. "It was over long ago. I'm not like that—not any more."

"Everybody's record has much worse comments

from the psychology majors," Kirk said. "Luckily for us, nobody ever reads ours. Pretend you didn't hear. Mr. Spock, any functional and motivating data on the life force?"

"I have asked the computer why these beings pursue the *Enterprise*. The first answer was 'Completion.' When I requested an alternate formulation, it gave me 'Fulfillment' instead. I find both responses unclear, but the machine has insufficient data to give us anything better, thus far."

The door opened and a yeoman entered with a cartridge which he handed to McCoy. The surgeon inserted it into his viewer. Almost at once, he cast a disturbed look at Mira.

"What is it, Doctor?"

"A comparison of our Steinman with Starfleet records shows that Lt. Romaine's fingerprints, voice analysis, reintal patterns, all external factors are the same as before. But according to the two encephalograms, her brain wave pattern has been altered."

"Isn't that impossible?" Kirk asked.

"That's what I was taught. The BCP is as consistent as fingerprints."

"Let's see it."

McCoy put the tape deck into the slot on the desk, and the tri-screen lit up. They all looked at it for a moment. Then Spock said, "Doctor, I believe that's the wrong slide."

"No it isn't, Spock. It's from tape deck D—brain circuitry pattern of Lt. Mira Romaine."

"No, Doctor. It happens to be tape deck H—the impulse tracking we obtained on the alien life units."

"Nurse Chapel followed this every step of the way. There can't be an error."

Mira was staring in tense horror at the screen.

"According to your records, Dr. McCoy," Spock said, "Lt. Romaine did not show abnormal telepathatic ability."

"That's right, Spock. Exceptional pliancy *was* indicated. It might be a factor."

"It must be. There is an identity of pattern between

these alien life forms and the mind of Lt. Romaine. Their thoughts are becoming her thoughts."

Scott said: "Mira's tried to tell me all along that she was seeing things happen in advance—"

"Why didn't you report it?" Kirk said.

"You don't report space sickness. That's all I ever thought it was."

"What else did she see?"

Scott thought a moment. "The first attack on the ship . . . the attack on Memory Alpha . . . and—the time we almost lost her."

"Those were all acts carried out by our attacker. Anything else?"

Scott got up and went over to Mira, who was still staring at the screen. "I thought there was another time. I guess I was wrong."

"Was he wrong, Lieutenant?" Kirk said.

Mira finally looked up at Scotty, who sank to one knee beside her. In a trancelike voice, she said, "Yes. There was one other time."

"What did you see?"

"I saw Scotty," she said, still looking at him intently.

"Where?"

"I don't know."

"What was he doing?"

"He was dying." Her hand went to Scott's face. "Now I understand what's been happening. I've been seeing through another mind. I have been flooded by thoughts that are not my own . . . by desires and drives that control me—" Suddenly she broke completely and was in Scott's arms. "Scotty—I would rather die than hurt you. I would rather die!"

"What's all this talk of dying?" Scott demanded. "They've called the turn on us three out of four times. That's a better average than anybody deserves. It's our turn now. We'll fight them. So let's not hear anything more about dying."

It was a bold speech, but Kirk could think of no way that the *Enterprise* could back it up. He punched the intercom. "Ensign Chekov, what success have you had with the evasive tactics?"

"Useless, sir. They'll probably be through the shields again in a minute or so."

Kirk turned to Mira. "They may destroy you and us as they did Memory Alpha. You are especially susceptible to their will. There is one way we might survive. Do not resist. Let them begin to function through you. If we can control that moment, we have a chance. Will you try?"

"Tell me what to do," she said, her voice shaky.

"Everybody down to the antigrav test unit. Follow me."

"Attention all personnel!" Sulu's voice barked from the intercom. "Clear all decks! Alien being has penetrated ship!"

The door to the gravity chamber opened off the interior of the medical lab. As the group from the Briefing Room entered at a run, Kirk said, "As soon as she enters the chamber, secure all ports."

But as Mira started for the chamber, the swirling colors of the life force pervaded the lab. She stopped and spun around, her hand going to her brow, her eyes blazing, her face contorted with struggle. Scott started toward her.

"Don't touch me!" It was a piercing scream. "Scotty—stay away—"

The multicolored flashes slowly and finally were gone, leaving Mira standing as if frozen. Then her lips parted, and from them came once more the sound of the unknown language.

"We've lost her to them," Scott said desperately, starting toward her once more.

"Stay where you are!" Kirk said.

McCoy added, "She could kill us all in this state."

"She will," Spock said, "unless we are able to complete what the Captain is planning."

Scott was looking at Mira in agony. "Stay with us, Mira. Stay with us, Mira Romaine!"

"I am trying," she said. It was her own voice, but

coming out in smothered gasps. "I want to be . . . with you . . . They are too strong."

"Fight them now, Mira," Kirk said. "Don't lose yourself to them. Hold on."

The girl sank against the door to the gravity chamber. Her eyes closed, her body became taut with the effort at control.

"I am Mira Romaine," she said, and this time her voice was angry. "I will be who I choose to be. Let me go!"

But the struggle was too much for her. Her body went limp, and her eyes opened, inexpressibly sad. In a voice like a lost soul, utterly unlike anything she had ever sounded before, she said:

"She cannot prevent us. You cannot stop us."

Scott lunged forward, but Kirk grabbed him. "Mira! Mira!"

"That's not Mira talking," McCoy said.

"Captain, we must deal with them directly," Spock said. "Now, while she retains partial identity, we can speak to them. Her voice will answer for them."

"I am the commander of this vessel," Kirk said to the entranced girl. "Do you understand me?"

"We understand you. We have searched for a millennium to find the One through whom we can see and hear and speak and live out our lives."

"Who are you?"

"We are of Zetar."

"All humanoid life on Zetar," Spock said, "was destroyed long ago."

"Yes. All corporeal life was destroyed."

"Then what are you?" Kirk demanded.

"The desires, the hopes, the thoughts and the will of the last hundred from Zetar. The force of life in us could not be wiped out."

"All things die."

"At the proper time. Our planet was dying. We were determined to live on. At the peak of our plans to go elsewhere, a sudden final disaster struck us down. But the force of our lives survived. And now at last we have found the One through whom we can live it out."

"The body you inhabit has its own life to lead."

"She will accept ours."

"She does not wish it. She is fighting to retain her own identity."

"Her mind will accept our thoughts. Our lives will be fulfilled."

"Will she learn like the people on Memory Alpha learned?"

"We did not wish to kill."

"You did kill!"

"No! Resisting us killed those on Memory Alpha. We did not kill. We wanted only the technician, but she fought back."

"The price of your survival is too high."

"We wish only the girl."

"You cannot have her," Kirk said fiercely. "You are entitled to your own lives. But you cannot have another's!"

Mira herself seemed to hear this, and her eyes to respond. When she spoke again, the voice was her own. "Life was given to *me*. It is mine. I will live it out—I will . . ."

Her voice weakened, and she sank back. McCoy took a tricorder reading. "The girl's life reading is becoming a match to the—Zetarians," he said. "She is losing."

"Do not fight us."

"They will not accept their own deaths," Spock said.

"They will be forced to accept it," Kirk said.

"You will all die," said the Mira/Zetar voice.

"Captain," Spock said, "unless we can complete the plan at once, they will carry out their threat."

McCoy said, "Jim, you realize that the pressure you need to kill the Zetarians might kill her, too?"

"At least, our way she has a chance. We must get her into the antigrav chamber."

They all moved in about her, in a close circle. Scott

forced himself to the front and said, "Mira will not kill me."

He stooped and quickly picked her up in his arms. He faced the opening to the gravity chamber, and his head snapped back, his face contorted in agony. Nevertheless he got her into the chamber, and the doors closed behind her. Then he crumpled to the floor. His face now, however, was relaxed. As McCoy bent over him, his eyes opened.

"I knew she wouldn't kill me," he said, with a faint smile.

Kirk and Spock went to the chamber's console, joined after a moment by McCoy. After a sweeping glance, Kirk then crossed to the bull's-eye port which gave visual access to the chamber.

"Neutralize gravity, Mr. Spock."

Mira's body lay on the floor of the chamber where Scott had put it for what seemed to be a long time. Then she moved feebly, and the motion set her to drifting weightlessly.

"The Zetarians are growing stronger," McCoy said. "The weightless state is their natural condition, after all."

"Begin pressurizing," Kirk said. "Bring it up to two atmospheres."

Spock turned a rheostat slowly. There seemed to be no change in Mira. Theoretically, there should begin to be some sort of feedback system going into operation between Mira's nervous system, as it responded to pressures on her body not natural to her, and the occupying wave patterns of the Zetarian brain; but no such effect was evident yet.

"Two atmospheres, Captain."

"Increase at the rate of one atmosphere a minute."

"Wait a minute, Jim," McCoy said. "Not even a deep-sea diver experiences pressure increases at that rate. They take it slowly, a few atmospheres at a time."

"That's just what I'm counting on, Bones. If it's something Mira can adapt to, there'll be no adverse effect on her, and hence none on them. Run it up as ordered, Mr. Spock."

His hands darting, Spock tied the pressure rheostat into circuit with a timer. "Rising now as ordered, Captain."

A quick glance at the big bourdon gauge showed this. Kirk glued his face back to the glass.

Still nothing seemed to be happening, except that Mira's head was now lolling from side to side.

"Jim, you're going to kill her at this rate!"

Kirk did not respond. The chamber was beginning to look hazy, as though water were beginning to condense out of the atmosphere inside it—but that couldn't be, because water vapor didn't condense except to a *decrease* in pressure—

The fogginess increased, and became luminescent. In a moment more, the chamber was pulsating with the multiple lights of the Zetar life force. It grew brighter and brighter for several seconds.

"Jim, you can't—"

Kirk silenced the surgeon with a savage gesture. Almost at the same moment, the lights vanished, and with them the fog.

"Cut, Spock!"

There was the snap of a toggle. Mira's eyes were now open. She looked entirely normal, though a little bewildered at finding herself floating in midair. Scott snatched up the microphone which fed the intercom in the tank.

"Don't move, Mira! It's going to be all right! They're gone—they're gone!"

Kirk turned away and gestured to McCoy to take over.

"Reduce pressure very *very* gradually, Mr. Spock," the surgeon said.

"It will tax Mr. Scott's patience, Doctor."

"We have all the time in the world, now," Scott said, his eyes glowing.

"Precisely," McCoy said. "And after all this, we don't want to lose the subject to a simple case of the bends. Lieutenant, lie perfectly still; you're in free fall and the slightest movement may bounce you off the chamber walls—and I don't want even the slightest bruise. Don't move at all, just take deep regular breaths . . . that's it . . . Mr. Spock, restore gravity very gradually. I want her to ground without even a jar . . . Mira, don't hold your breath. Breathe deeply and continuously . . . That's it—in, out, in, out, keep it steady . . . Fine. You won't be out of there for another two hours, so you might as well relax. The battle's over, anyhow."

There was a deep sigh all around. Perhaps Mira had given up holding her breath, but it was evident that she had not been alone.

"Spock," Kirk said, "is it possible for you to judge the long-range mental effects on the Lieutenant?"

"I am not an expert, Captain, and bear in mind that Lt. Romaine's mind was invaded by something quite inhuman. However, despite Starfleet's judgment of her pliancy, she put up a valiant struggle to retain her identity. I would propose that that augurs well."

"Spock is right, Jim," McCoy said, to Kirk's surprise. "While the truth was hard for her to take, when it was brought out, the girl reacted well. The struggle she put up in this experience, I would say, will strengthen her whole ego structure."

"Would either of you credit Scotty's steadfast belief in her as a factor?"

Spock's eyebrow arched suspiciously. "You mean 'love' as a motivation? Humans claim a great deal for that particular emotion. It is possible, but—"

"No 'buts' at all," McCoy said. "It was a deciding factor—and will be, in the girl's recovery."

"Then, do I understand you both agree that Lt. Romaine need not return to Starbase for further treatment?"

"I would say," Spock said, "that work is the better therapy."

"Absolutely, Jim."

"Scotty, unsmash your nose from that port and give us a sober opinion. How is Lt. Romaine now?"

"Beautiful, Captain."

"Ready to return to work?"

"Positively, Captain."

There was an exchange of grins all around. Then Kirk turned to the intercom. "Kirk to bridge."

"Sulu here, Captain."

"Set course for Memory Alpha. Lt. Romaine has lots of work to do there."

THE APPLE

(Max Ehrlich and Gene L. Coon)

Even from orbit, Gamma Trianguli VI seemed both beautiful and harmless, as close to an earthly paradise as the *Enterprise* had ever encountered. Such planets were more than rare, and Kirk thought for a few moments that he might have happened upon a colonizable world—until the sensors indicated that there was already native humanoid life there.

He duly reported the facts to Starfleet Command, who seemed to be as impressed as he was. Their orders were to investigate the planet and its culture. Under the circumstances, Kirk ordered a landing party of six: himself, Spock, Chekov, Yeoman Martha Landon, and two security guards, Marple and Kaplan.

Carrying tricorders and specimen bags, the party materialized in what might almost have been a garden. Large exotic flowers grew in profusion, and there were heavily laden fruit trees. Here and there, outcroppings of rainbow-colored rock competed with the floral hues, and over it all stretched a brilliant, cloudless day. Feeling a sudden impulse to share all this beauty as widely as possible, Kirk called down McCoy and two more security guards—Mallory and Hendorf, as it turned out.

McCoy looked around appreciatively. "I might just put in a claim for all this and settle down."

"I doubt that the natives would approve, Bones," Kirk said. "But it is pretty spectacular."

"A shame we have to intrude."

"We do what Starfleet tells us."

Spock, who had knelt to inspect the soil, arose. "Remarkably rich and fertile, Captain. Husbandry would be quite efficacious here."

"You're sure about that?" Kirk said, amused without quite knowing why.

"Quite sure. Our preliminary readings indicate the entire planet is covered by growth like this. Quite curious. Even at the poles there is only a slight variation in temperature, which maintains a planet-wide average of seventy-six degrees."

"I know," Kirk said. "Meteorologically, that's almost impossible."

"It makes me homesick, Captain," Chekov said. "Just like Russia."

"It's a lot more like the Garden of Eden, Ensign," McCoy said.

"Of course, Doctor. The Garden of Eden was just outside Moscow. A very nice place. It must have made Adam and Eve very sad to leave."

Kirk stared at him; Chekov seemed completely straight-faced and earnest. Was this just another of his outbreaks of Russian patriotism, or some side effect of his developing romance with Yeoman Landon? "All right. There's a village about seventeen kilometers away on bearing two thirty-two. We'll head that way."

"Captain!" The call had come from Hendorf, who was examining one of the plants: a small bush with large pods, at the center of each of which was a cluster of sharp, thick thorns. "Take a look at—"

With only a slight puff of noise, one of the pods exploded. Hendorf staggered and looked down at his chest. Perhaps a dozen thorns were sticking in a neat group near his heart. He opened his mouth in an attempt to speak, and then collapsed.

McCoy was there first, but only a quick examination was needed. "He's dead."

"What was all that about Paradise?" Kirk said grimly. He took out his communicator. "Kirk to *Enterprise* . . . Mr. Scott, we've already had a casualty. Hendorf has been killed by a poisonous plant at these coordinates. As soon as we've moved out of the way, beam up his body."

"Aye, Captain. That's a shame about Hendorf." Scott paused a moment. "We seem to have a little problem up here, too. We're losing potency in the antimatter banks. I don't think it's serious, but we're looking into it."

"What's causing it?"

"We're not sure. We've run measurements of the electromagnetic field of the planet, and they're a wee bit abnormal. Could have something to do with it."

"Well, stay on top of it. Kirk out."

"I find that odd, Captain," Spock said.

"So do I. But Scotty'll find the problem. Turn up anything with your tricorder?"

"Indeed, sir. Most puzzling. There are strong vibrations under the surface, for miles in every direction."

"Subsurface water?"

"I don't believe so. They are quite strong and reasonably regular. Though I have no evidence to support it, I feel that they are artificially produced. I will, of course, continue to investigate."

"Of course. It may tie in with Scotty's trouble. Ensign Mallory, we'll be heading for the village. Go ahead and scout it out. Avoid contact with the humanoids, but get us a complete picture. And be careful. There may be other dangers besides poisonous plants. Keep in constant communicator touch."

"Aye aye, sir."

Spock held up a hand and froze. "Captain," he said, very softly. "I hear something . . ." He swung his tricorder. "Humanoid . . . a few feet away . . . moving with remarkable agility . . . bearing eighteen."

Kirk made a quick, surreptitious gesture to the two remaining security guards, who nodded and disappeared in opposite directions in the brush. Kirk moved cautiously forward along the bearing. But there was nobody there. Puzzled, he turned back.

"What is it?" Chekov said.

"A visitor," Spock said. "One wanting to retain his anonymity, I would say."

Martha Landon, who had been sticking close to Chekov throughout, shivered.

"What's the matter?"

"Oh, nothing, I suppose," the girl said. "But . . . all this beauty . . . and now Mr. Hendorf dead, somebody watching us. It's frightening."

"If you insist on worrying, worry about me," Chekov said. "I've been wanting to get you in a place like this for a long time."

She beamed at him; obviously nothing could make her happier. Kirk said sharply: "Mr. Chekov, Yeoman Landon, I know you find each other fascinating, but we did not come here to carry out a field experiment in human biology. If you please—"

"Of course, Captain," Chekov said, hurriedly breaking out his tricorder. "I was just about to take some readings."

Kirk rejoined Spock and McCoy, shaking his head. "Nothing. Whoever it is, it moves like a cat."

"Jim, I don't like this."

"Neither do I, Bones, but we have an assignment to carry out. All hands. We've been watched, and we'll probably be watched. Move out—formation D—no stragglers."

The start of the maneuver brought Spock to an outcropping of the rainbow-colored rock. He picked up a piece, studied it, and applied slight pressure. The lump broke into two unequal parts.

"Most interesting. Extremely low specific gravity. Some uraninite, hornblende, quartz—but a number of other compounds I cannot immediately identify. An analysis should be interesting."

He tucked the smaller portion into his specimen bag, and tossed the larger piece away. When it hit the ground, there was a small but violent explosion.

Kirk, shaken, looked around, but no one had been

hurt. "You wouldn't mind being a little more careful where you throw rocks, Mr. Spock?"

Spock stared at the outcropping. "Fascinating. Obviously highly unstable. Captain, if indeed this material is as abundant elsewhere as it is here, this is a find of some importance. A considerable source of power."

"Humph. A Garden of Eden—with land mines." His communicator buzzed. "Kirk here. What is it, Scotty?"

"Our antimatter banks are completely inert. I couldn't stop it. But I found out why. There's a transmission of some sort, a beam, from the surface. It affects antimatter like a pail of water on a fire. We're trying to analyze it, but it pinpoints in the area of the village you're approaching, so maybe you could act more effectively from down there."

"We'll try. Kirk out . . . Mr. Spock, could this correlate with the vibrations you detected? A generator of some kind?"

"Possibly. If so, an immense one. And undoubtably subterranean—*Jim!*"

With a shout, Spock leapt forward and knocked Kirk to the ground. When Kirk got back to his feet, more astonished than angry, Spock was staring at a dozen thorns neatly imbedded in his chest. Then the Vulcan slowly crumpled and fell.

"Spock! McCoy, do something!"

McCoy was already there. "Still alive." He dipped into his kit, came up with his air hypo, inserted a cartridge and gave Spock a shot, seemingly all in one smooth motion. Then, after a moment, he looked up at Kirk. "Not responding, Jim. We'll have to get him to the ship."

"And not just him. We're overextended." Kirk took out his communicator. "Scotty? We're beaming back up, all of us. Notify the Transporter Room. And make arrangements to pick up Ensign Mallory; he's scouting ahead of us."

"Aye aye, sir . . . Transporter Room, stand by to beam up landing party . . . Standing by, Captain."

"Energize."

The sparkle of the Transporter effect began around them. The surroundings started to fade out . . . and then wavered, reappeared, faded, reappeared and stabilized.

"Mr. Scott! What's wrong?"

"No Transporter contact, Captain. The entire system seems to be inhibited. The way it is now, we couldna beam up a fly."

"Any connection with the warp drive malfunction?"

"I dinna ken, skipper, but I'll check on it, and get back to you. Scott out."

Kirk started to turn back to McCoy, then halted with astonishment as he saw Spock stirring. The Vulcan sat up weakly, looking distinctly off his normal complexion.

"Spock!"

"I am quite all right, Captain . . . A trifle dizzy . . ."

"Bones?"

"It must be hard to poison that green Vulcan blood. And then there was the shot. I guess he just took a while bouncing back."

"Just what did you think you were doing?" Kirk demanded, helping Spock up.

"I saw that you were unaware of that plant, so I—"

"So you took the thorns yourself!"

"I assure you I had no intention of doing so. My own clumsiness prevented me from moving out of the way."

"I can jump out of the way as well as the next man. Next time you're not to get yourself killed. Do you know how much money Starfleet has invested in you?"

"Certainly. In training, fifteen thousand, eight hundred a year; in pay up to last month—"

"Never mind, Spock. But . . . thanks."

"Jim," McCoy said, "the more I think about this place, the more I get an idea that . . . Well, it's kind of far out, but . . ."

"Go on, Bones."

"Well, when bacteria invade a human body, the

white corpuscles hurry to the invasion point and try to destroy the invader. The mind isn't conscious of it. The body just does it."

"You might be right, Bones. Not only is something after us, but I think it's also after the ship."

Spock shook his head. "To affect the ship at this extreme range, Captain, would require something like a highly sophisticated planetary defense system. It would hardly seem possible—"

He stopped as the group was suddenly enveloped in shadow. They turned as one and stared at the sky. Great towering masses of storm clouds were gathering there. It was impossible; thirty seconds ago the sky had been cloudless. An ominous rumble confirmed that the impossible was indeed happening.

With a deafening clap of thunder, a jagged, blue-white stab of lightning flashed in their midst, tumbling them all like ninepins.

Then the shadow lifted. Kirk got up cautiously. At the spot where the security guard named Kaplan had been standing, there was now only a spot of charred, smoking earth. Helpless, at a loss for words, furious, Kirk stared at it, and then back at the sky as Spock joined him.

"A beautiful day, Mr. Spock," Kirk said bitterly. "Not a cloud in the sky. Just like Paradise."

His communicator beeped. "Mallory here, Captain. I'm near the village. Coordinates one-eighteen by two-twenty. The village is—" Mallory's voice was interrupted by a blast of static.

"What was that, Mallory? I don't read you."

"I'm getting static too. I said it's primitive—strictly tribal from the looks of it. But there's something else—"

Another tearing squeal of static. Mallory's voice stopped. Kirk could not get him back.

"Captain," Spock said, "those coordinates were only a few thousand meters off that way."

"Let's go! On the double!"

They crashed off. As they broke out of the other side of the undergrowth, Kirk saw Mallory running toward them over a field littered with rainbow-colored rocks.

"Over there, Captain," the security guard shouted. "It's—"

He had turned his head as he ran, to point. It was impossible to tell exactly what happened next. Perhaps he stubbed his toe. A rock exploded directly under him.

By the time they reached him, no check by McCoy was needed. His body lay unmoving, bloody, broken.

Kirk, shaken, closed his eyes for a moment. First Hendorf, then Kaplan. He had known Kaplan's family. And Mallory . . . Mallory's father had helped Kirk into the Academy . . .

Spock took his arm, waving the others off.

"Captain . . . in each case, it was unavoidable."

"You're wrong, Spock. I should have beamed us all up the minute things started to go wrong."

"You were under orders. You had no choice."

"I could have saved two men at least. Beamed up. Made further investigations from the ship. Done something! This . . . blundering along down here . . . cut off from the ship . . . the ship's in trouble itself . . . unable to help it . . ."

"We can help it, Captain. The source of the interference with the ship must be here on the planet. Indeed, this may be the only place the difficulty can be solved."

"And how many more lives will I lose?"

"No one has ever stated Starfleet duty was particularly safe. You have done everything a commander could do. I believe—" He broke off, listening. "Captain . . . I think our visitor is back again."

Reluctantly, Kirk turned to Marple, the last of the security guards of the landing party. "Ensign, go ahead fifty yards, swing to your left, cut back, and make a lot of noise. Mr. Spock, Mr. Chekov, make a distraction, a loud one."

He moved quietly away from them toward the brush. Behind him, Chekov's voice rose: "What kind of a tricorder setting do you call that?"

"I will not have you speaking to me in that tone of voice, Ensign!"

"Well, what do you want, violins? That's the stupidest setting I've ever seen—and you a Science Officer!"

Kirk crept stealthily forward.

"It's time you paid more attention to your own duties," Spock's voice shouted uncharacteristically. "Furthermore, you are down here to work, not to hold hands with a pretty yeoman!"

There was somebody, or something, ahead now. Kirk parted the brush. Directly in front of him, his back turned, was a small humanoid, his skin copper red, his hair platinum blond. There seemed to be two tiny silver studs behind his ears. Kirk tensed himself to spring.

At the same time, Marple came crashing toward them from the opposite side. The alien sprang up and ran directly into Kirk's arms. The alien struggled. Measuring him coolly, Kirk struck him squarely on the jaw, and he went down. Clutching his face, he began to cry like a child.

Kirk stood over him, slowly relaxing. Obviously, this creature was no threat. "I'm not going to hurt you," he said. "Do you understand? I won't hurt you."

He spoke, without much hope, in Interstellar. To his surprise, the alien responded in the same tongue, though much slurred and distorted.

"You struck me with your hand."

"I won't strike you again. Here." Kirk extended his hand to help the being up. After a moment, the hand was taken. "You've been following us, watching us. Why?"

"I am the Eyes of Vaal. He must see."

"Who is Vaal?"

"Vaal is Vaal. He is everything."

"You have a name?"

"I am Akuta. I lead the Feeders of Vaal."

The rest of the party began to gather around them. Akuta tried to flinch in all directions at once.

"They won't hurt you either. I promise. Akuta, we

have come here in peace. We would like to speak to your Vaal."

"Akuta alone speaks to Vaal. I am the eyes and the voice of Vaal. It is his wish."

"This is fascinating," Spock said. He stepped forward and put his hands gently to Akuta's head, turning it slightly for a closer look at the two small metal studs. "If you will permit me, sir . . . Captain, observe."

"Antennae?" Kirk said.

Akuta had suffered the examination without protest. "They are my ears for Vaal. They were given to me in the dim time, so the people could understand his commands, and obey."

"The people," Kirk said. "Are they nearby?"

"We are close to Vaal, so we may serve him. I shall take you there."

Kirk's communicator shrilled. "Kirk here."

It was Scott: "Captain, something's grabbed us from the planet's surface! Like a giant tractor beam! We can't break loose—we can't even hold our own."

"Warp drive still out?"

"Yes, Captain. All we have is impulse power, and that on maximum. Even with that, we'll only be able to maintain power for sixteen hours. Then we'll burn up for sure."

"Mr. Scott, you are my Chief Engineer. You know everything about that ship there is to know . . . more than the men who designed it. If you can't get those warp engines going again—you're fired."

"I'll try everything there is to try, sir. Scott out."

Kirk turned to Akuta. "Tell me about Vaal."

"All the world knows about Vaal. He makes the rains fall, and the sun to shine. All good comes from Vaal."

"Take us to him. We want to speak with him."

"I will take you, but Vaal will not speak with you. He speaks only to me."

"We'll take our chances."

Nodding, Akuta led the way.

Vaal became visible from a clearing some distance away. He was a great serpentlike head, seeming to have been cut out of a cliff. His mouth was open. In color it was greenish bronze, except for its red tongue, which extended from its open mouth. There were steps cut in the tongue, so that a man could walk right up and into the mouth. Two huge fangs extended down, white and polished. Vaal's eyes were open, and they glowed dimly red, pulsating regularly. Even from here, they could hear that the pulsation was timed with a faint but powerful-sounding low-pitched hum.

They drew closer, both Spock and Chekov taking tricorder readings. "Of a high order of workmanship, and very ancient," the First Officer said.

"But this isn't the center, Spock," Kirk said.

"No, Captain. The center is deep beneath it. This would seem to be an access point. In addition there is an energy field extending some thirty feet beyond the head in all directions. Conventional in composition, but most formidable."

"Akuta, how do you talk to Vaal?"

"Vaal calls me. Only then."

Kirk turned to the rest of the party, scowling. "Well, we can't get to it, and we can't talk to it until it's ready to talk."

"Vaal sleeps now," Akuta said. "When he is hungry, you may be able to talk with him—if he desires it."

"When does he get hungry?"

"Soon. Come. We will give you food and drink. If you are tired, you may rest."

He led them down the hill and back into the jungle. It was not very long before they emerged in a tiny village, which looked part Polynesian, part American Indian, part exotic in its own way. There were small thatched huts with hanging batik tapestries, simply made and mostly repeating the totem image of Vaal. At one end of the village area were neatly stacked piles of the explosive rainbow-colored rock. About a dozen aliens were there, men and women, all very handsome, all younger than Akuta. They seemed to be doing nothing at all.

"Akuta," Kirk said, "where are the others?"

"There are no others."

"But . . . where are the children?"

"Children? You speak unknown words to me."

"Little people," Kirk explained. "Like yourselves. But they grow."

"Ah," said Akuta. "Replacements. None are necessary. They are forbidden by Vaal."

"But," said Martha Landon, "when people fall in love—" Chekov was standing next to her, and at these words he smiled and slipped his hand around her waist. She pressed it to her.

"Strange words," said Akuta. "Children . . . love. What is love?"

"Well . . . when a man and a woman are . . . attracted . . ." She did not seem to be able to go any farther. Akuta stared at her and at Chekov's arm.

"Ah. The holding. The touching. Vaal has forbidden this."

"There goes Paradise," said Chekov.

During the questioning, the People of Vaal had been drawing closer and closer, not menacingly, but in simple curiosity. Akuta turned to them.

"These are strangers from another place. They have come among us. Welcome them."

A young man stepped forward, beaming. "Welcome to Vaal."

A girl, beautiful as a goddess, though wearing slightly less, stepped out with a lei of flowers in her hands, smiling warmly. She went to Kirk and put the lei over his head. "Our homes are open to you."

Thus encouraged, the others came over, giggling, touching, exploring, examining the clothing and the gadgets of the strangers. Another young woman put a necklace of shells around Spock's neck.

"It does something for you, Mr. Spock," Kirk said.

"Indeed, Captain. It makes me most uncomfortable."

"I am Sayana," the girl said. "You have a name?"

"I am Spock."

Sayana repeated the name, pointing to him, and so did the rest of the natives, with a wave of laughter.

"I fail to see," Spock said, "what they find so amusing."

"Come," said Akuta. He led the landing party off to one of the huts. The rest of the People of Vaal continued to crowd around, laughing and probing gently.

The interior of the hut was simple, indeed primitive. There were a few baskets, a few wooden vessels, some hangings with the totem image on them, sleeping mats on the floor.

"This house is your house," Akuta said. "I will send food and drink. You are welcome in the place of Vaal."

He went out. Chekov stared after him. "Now we're welcome. A while ago this whole planet was trying to kill us. It doesn't make sense."

"Nothing does down here," McCoy agreed. "I'm going to run a physiological reading on some of those villagers."

He went out after Akuta. Kirk took out his communicator. "Kirk to *Enterprise*. Come in."

"Scott here, sir."

"Status report, Scotty."

"No change, Captain. The orbit is decaying along the computed lines. No success with the warp drive. We're going down and we can't stop it."

"I'm sick of hearing that word 'can't,' Scott," Kirk said harshly. "Get my ship out of there."

"But, sir—we've tried everything within engineering reason—"

"Then use your imagination! Tie every dyne of power the ship has into the impulse engines. Discard the warp drive nacelles if you have to and crack out of there with just the main section—but get out!"

"Well, we could switch over all but the life support circuits and boost the impulse power—black the ship out otherwise—"

"Do it. Kirk out."

McCoy reentered, frowning. "Incredible," he said. "I

ran a complete check on the natives. There's a complete absence of harmful bacteria in their systems. No tissue degeneration, no calcification, no arteriosclerosis. In simple terms, they're not growing old. I can't begin to tell you how old any of them are. Twenty years—or twenty thousand."

"Quite possible," Spock said. "It checks with my atmosphere analysis. The atmosphere completely screens out all dangerous radiation from their sun."

"Add to that a simple diet," Kirk said, "perfectly controlled temperature . . . apparently no vices at all . . . no natural enemies . . . and no 'replacements' needed. Maybe it is Paradise, after all—for them."

Outside, there was a curious vibrating sound, not loud, but penetrating, like the striking of an electronic gong. Kirk went out, beckoning to Spock.

The People of Vaal were no longer lounging around. They were moving off toward the cliff, picking up rocks from the stockpiles as they left. Kirk and Spock followed.

At the cliff, the people entered the mouth of Vaal with the rocks, and came out without them. The red eyes were flashing, brightly now.

"Apparently our hypothesis is correct," Spock said. "There is no living being in there. It is a machine, nothing more."

"The field's down. The people are going in. Let's see what luck we have."

Kirk took a step forward. There was an immediate rumble of thunder, to the considerable alarm of the People of Vaal. Kirk stepped back quickly. "That's not the way."

"Evidently not. It is no ordinary machine, Captain. It has shown a capacity for independent action in its attacks upon us. It may well possess a more than rudimentary intelligence."

"But it needs to eat. It can't have any great power reserves."

"Indeed, Captain. But that does not seem to be of help. The ship now has only ten hours to break free."

"What if Vaal's power weakens as it approaches

feeding time? Mr. Spock, check with the ship; get an estimate of the total energy being expended against it. And measure it every hour."

"With pleasure, Captain." Spock took his communicator out quickly. Deep in thought, Kirk went back to the hut, where he found all of the landing party outside.

"What was it, Jim?"

"Mess call, Bones."

Spock came up behind him. "A perfect example of symbiosis. They provide for Vaal, and Vaal gives them everything they need."

"Which may also answer why there are no children here," Kirk said. "There are exactly enough people to do what Vaal requires."

"In my view," Spock said, "a splendid example of reciprocity."

"It would take a mind like yours to make that kind of statement," McCoy said.

"Gentlemen, your arguments can wait until the ship is out of danger."

"Jim," McCoy said, "you can't just blind yourself to what is happening here. These are humanoids—intelligent! They've got to advance—progress! Don't you understand what my readings indicate? There's been no change here in perhaps thousands of years! This isn't life, it's stagnation!"

"You are becoming emotional, Doctor," Spock said. "This seems to be a perfectly practical society."

"Practical? It's obscene! Humanoids living only so that they can service a hunk of tin!"

"A remarkable hunk of tin, Bones," Kirk said. "And they seem healthy and happy."

"That has nothing to do with it—"

Kirk's communicator cut in. "Kirk here."

"Scott, sir. We've got a reading on the power source as Spock asked. It *is* dropping a bit at a time—nominal, but a definite drain."

Kirk grinned triumphantly at Spock. "Good. Keep monitoring. How are you doing with the circuit switchover?"

"We're putting everything but the kitchen sink into the impulse drive, sir. It'll take another eight hours to complete the work."

"That's cutting it fine, Scotty."

"Aye, sir. But if we don't break out, I'd rather we didn't have to wait long for the end of it."

Kirk took a deep breath. "Right. Carry on, Scotty. Kirk out."

The hours wore away. A large assortment of fruit and vegetables was brought to the landing party by the People. Martha Landon was nervous and on the verge of tears; Kirk sent her out with Chekov for "a breath of air" and whatever reassurance Chekov could give her. Privately, Kirk hoped also that the People would spy on them; the sight of a little open necking might give them a few ideas disruptive to the absolute control Vaal had over them. Of course, that might provoke Vaal to retaliation—but what more could Vaal do than he was doing now?

Spock seemed to read Kirk's intentions with no difficulty. "I am concerned, Captain," he said. "This may not be an ideal society, but it is a viable one. If we are forced to do what it seems we must, in my opinion, we will be in direct violation of the noninterference directive."

"I'm not convinced that this is a viable society in the accepted sense of the word. Bones was right. These people aren't living, they're just existing. It's not a valid culture."

"Starfleet Command may think otherwise."

"That's a risk I'll have to take." He called the *Enterprise*. "How's it coming, Scotty?"

"Almost ready, sir. We'll need a half hour yet."

"You've only got forty-five minutes until you're pulled into the atmosphere."

"I know, sir. As you said, it's cutting things a bit fine."

"I think we're going to be able to help down here. I'll be back in touch shortly." Kirk cut off. "All hands. We're coming up on the next feeding time for Vaal.

Before that happens I want all the Vaalians confined in one hut—the women too, no exceptions. When that gong sounds, round them all up."

The gong in fact sounded only a few minutes later. By this time Chekov and McCoy, phasers drawn, had herded all the People together. They milled around inside the hut, appalled, some wailing and crying.

"Vaal calls us!" Akuta cried out. His face contorted in agony, and he touched the electrodes behind his ears. "We must go to him! He hungers!" The bell rang again. "Please! Let us go to him! We must!"

Kirk got out the communicator again. "Scotty, do you still have phaser power?"

"Aye sir. But what—"

"Lock all banks on the coordinates of the energy field you located down here. On my command, fire and maintain full phasers on those coordinates."

"Aye, sir, but they won't penetrate the field."

"If my guess is right, they won't have to. Stand by."

The bell rang again, louder, longer, more insistently. After checking to see that Chekov and McCoy had the People under control, Kirk and Spock went to the edge of the village. Spock pointed his tricorder toward the cliff.

"Interesting, Captain. The center of the emanations—Vaal—is somewhat weaker than the readings I've been getting. There are wide variations in energy transmission, as though it is drawing from other sources."

"Tapping its energy cells?"

"I would assume so."

"Right. I think the ship's attempts to pull away must have weakened it considerably. It needs to be fed, but the reserve capacity could hold out for days."

"If it has to reinforce its energy field to ward off a phaser attack, it will have to draw more heavily on its reserves."

"My plan exactly, Mr. Spock . . . Kirk to *Enterprise.* Open fire as ordered and maintain."

The phaser beams came down, in long sustained bursts. They were stopped short of the head of Vaal by the force field, but they continued to come down. Sparks flew at the point of contact. A hum rose from Vaal. loud and piercing.

"Tremendous upsurge in generated power, sir. Obviously Vaal is trying to reinforce its energy field."

"Good. Let's see how long it can do it!"

The sky darkened. A strong wind began to blow. Strong flashes of lights lit up Vaal's maw, and some smoke began to appear. The hum was now intolerably loud, and the wind was howling. Lightning flashed overhead, followed by thunder. The din was terrific.

Then, almost all at once, the storm clouds dissipated, the flashes inside Vaal's mouth stopped, and its eyes went out. The hum too was gone.

"Kirk to *Enterprise*. Cease firing."

"No power generation at all," Spock said. "Vaal is dead."

"Mr. Scott, status report."

"Tractor beam gone. Potency returning to antimatter banks. I'll put all engineering sections on repairing the circuits immediately. We'll have the Transporter working in an hour."

Kirk felt as though a great weight had slid off his shoulders. "You're rehired, Mr. Scott. When the Transporter's fixed, form an engineering detail with full analytical equipment and beam them down. I think they'll find some interesting things inside that cave. Kirk out . . . Bones, Chekov. Let them out."

The People emerged, huddled, frightened, still sobbing. McCoy came over to Kirk and Spock.

"Allow me to point out, Captain," Spock said, "that by destroying Vaal, you have also destroyed the People of Vaal."

"Nonsense, Spock!" McCoy said. "It will be the making of these people. Make them stand on their own feet, do things for themselves. They have a right to live like men."

"You mean they have a right to pain, worry, insecurity, tension . . . and eventually death and taxes."

"That's all part of it. Yes! Those too!"

"I hope you will be able to find a way to explain it to them." He nodded toward Akuta, who had moved out of the group toward them, tears streaming down his face.

"Vaal is dead. You have killed him. We cannot live."

"You'll live, Akuta," Kirk said gently. "I'll assign some of my people here to help you."

The girl Sayana was crying quietly. One of the young men, standing by her, obviously wanted to comfort her, but did not know how to start. He made several ineffectual gestures; and then, as if by instinct, his arms went around her waist. She moved closer to him, and her head went onto his shoulder.

"But," Akuta said, "it was Vaal who put the fruit on the trees, who caused the rain to fall. Vaal cared for us."

"You'll find that putting fruit on the trees is a relatively simple matter. Our agronomist will help you with that. As for Vaal taking care of you, you'll have to learn to take care of yourselves. You might even like it.

"Listen to me, all of you. From this day on, you will not depend on Vaal. You are your own masters. You will be able to think what you wish, say what you wish, do what you wish. You will learn many things that are strange, but they will be good. You will discover love; there will be children."

"What are children?" Sayana said.

As the young man's arm tightened around her waist, Kirk grinned. "You just go on the way you're going, and you'll find out."

As Kirk, McCoy and Spock were going toward the bridge, McCoy said: "Spock has an interesting analogy, Captain."

"Yes, Mr. Spock?"

"I am not at all certain that we have done exactly the right thing on Gamma Trianguli VI, Captain."

"We put those people back on a normal course of social evolution. I see nothing wrong with that. It's a good object lesson, Spock, in what can happen when your machines become too efficient, do too much of your work for you. Judging by their language, those people must have been among the very first interstellar colonists—good hardy stock. They tamed the planet, instituted weather control, and turned all jobs of that sort over to a master computer, powered by the plentiful local ore. I suppose the fatal mistake was in giving the computer the power to program itself—and the end product was Vaal . . . Bones said something about an analogy."

"Perhaps you will recall the biblical story of Genesis, sir?"

"I recall it very well, Spock."

"We found a race of people living in Paradise, much as Adam and Eve did. They were obeying every word of Vaal. We taught them, in effect, to disobey that word. In a manner of speaking we have given Adam and Eve the apple . . . the awareness of good and evil, if you will . . . and because of this they have been driven out of Paradise."

Kirk stopped and swung around on Spock suspiciously. "Mr. Spock, you seem to be casting me in the role of Satan. Do I look like Satan?"

"No, sir. But—"

"Is there anyone on this ship who looks even remotely like Satan?"

McCoy was grinning broadly. "I am not aware," Spock said stiffly, "of anyone in that category, Captain."

"No, Mr. Spock. I didn't think you would be."

BY ANY OTHER NAME
(D. C. Fontana and Jerome Bixby)

The landing party answering the distress call consisted of Kirk, Spock, McCoy, the security officer Lt. Shea, and Yeoman Leslie Thompson. At first there seemed to be no source at all on the planet for the call—no wrecked spaceship, no debris. Had the ship been destroyed in space and the survivors proceeded here in a shuttle?

Then two people appeared from the nearby trees, a man and a woman, dressed in outfits rather like Merchant Marine jumpsuits. The woman was lovely, but it was the man who dominated their attention. He looked fortyish, with enormous power in his sturdy frame, great authority and competence in his bearing. Neither of the strangers seemed armed, but Kirk noticed that they wore small unobtrusive boxes on their belts. Their hands rested on the belts near the boxes in an attitude so casually assumed that it seemed to be only a part of their stance, but Kirk was wary.

"I'm Captain James Kirk of the USS *Enterprise*. We came in answer to your distress call."

"It was very kind of you to respond so quickly, Captain. But now you will surrender your ship to me."

Kirk stared. "You have an odd sense of humor."

The strangers touched buttons on the boxes. Instantly, Kirk found himself paralyzed—and so, evidently, was the rest of the "rescue" party.

"I am Rojan, of Kelva," the strange man said. "I am your Commander, from this moment on. Efforts to resist us, or to escape, will be severely punished. Soon we, and you, will leave this galaxy forever. You humans must face the end of your existence as you have known it."

The woman moved forward to relieve the people of the *Enterprise* of their phasers and communicators. Rojan went on: "You are paralyzed by a selective field that neutralizes impulses to the voluntary muscles. I will now release you all, Captain Kirk."

He touched the belt device. Kirk tensed to jump him, then thought better of it. "A neural field?"

"Radiated from a central projector, directed at whomever we wish."

"What do you want?"

"Your ship, Captain. We have monitored many. The *Enterprise*—a starship—is the best of its kind in your galaxy. It will serve us well in the long voyage that is to come."

"Voyage to where?"

"To your neighboring galaxy, in the constellation you call Andromeda."

"*Why?*"

"The Andromeda galaxy is our home," Rojan said in a remote voice.

"What brought you here?" Spock said.

"Within ten millennia, high radiation levels will make life in our galaxy impossible; it is reaching the stage in its evolution which will make it what you call a quasar. The Kelvan Empire sent forth ships to explore other galaxies—to search for one which our race could conquer and colonize."

"Sorry," Kirk said. "This galaxy is occupied."

"Captain, you think you are unconquerable—your ship impregnable. While we have talked, three of my people have boarded it, and the capture has begun." He took one of the confiscated communicators from the Kelvan woman and clicked it open. "Subcommander Hanar, report."

"This ship is ours," a strange voice said from the communicator. "We control the bridge, engineering and life support."

Rojan folded the communicator shut, and stowed it on his own belt.

"What good is capturing my ship?" Kirk said. "Even at maximum warp, the *Enterprise* couldn't get to the Andromeda galaxy for thousands of years. It's two million light-years away!"

"We will modify its engines to produce velocities far beyond the reach of your science. The journey between galaxies will take less than three hundred of your years."

"Fascinating," Spock said, "Intergalactic travel requiring 'only' three hundred years is a leap beyond anything man has yet accomplished."

Yeoman Thompson asked the Kelvan woman: "Did you make a voyage of three hundred years?"

"Our ships were of multigeneration design," the woman said. "I was born in the intergalactic void. I shall die there, during the return journey."

"Our mission," Rojan added, "will be completed by a Captain who will be my descendant."

"What happened to your ship?" Kirk said.

"There is an energy barrier at the rim of your galaxy—"

"I know. We've been there."

"We broke through it with great difficulty. Our ship was destroyed. We barely escaped in a life craft. Our time here has been spent scanning your systems, studying you. And now we have the means to begin our journey again."

"Why use our vessel?" Spock said. "Why not transmit a message back to your galaxy?"

"No form of transmission can penetrate the barrier."

"Rojan," Kirk said, "we could take your problem to our Federation. Research expeditions have catalogued hundreds of uninhabited planets in this galaxy. Surely some of them would be suitable for your colonization."

"We do not colonize, Captain," Rojan said sharply. "We conquer. We rule. There is no other way for us."

"In other words," McCoy said, 'this galaxy isn't big enough for both of us'?"

"What will happen to the intelligent races here?" Kirk said.

"They will not be mistreated. Merely subordinated." Rojan shrugged. "The fate of the inferior . . . in any galaxy. Ah, Hanar!"

While he had been speaking, another Kelvan had popped into being beside him, a younger man, with a hard intelligent face. There was no shimmer or any other such effect comparable to the workings of the Transporter; he just appeared.

"Tomar has examined the ship," Hanar said. "The modifications are under way."

"Space again!" said Rojan. "I don't think we could have kept our sanity, living so long on this accursed planet."

It did not seem to be so accursed to Kirk; in fact it was quite a pleasant, Earthlike place. But Hanar said: "It is an undisciplined environment; one cannot control it. Yet there are things of interest."

"Yes. But—disturbing. These ugly shells in which we have encased ourselves . . . they have such heightened senses. How do humans manage to exist in such fragile casings?"

They did not seem to care at all whether they were overheard, an obvious expression of supreme confidence. Kirk listened intently to every word; he had known such self-confidence to be misplaced before.

"Since the ship is designed to sustain this form," Hanar said, "we have little choice."

Rojan turned to the woman. "Kelinda, take them to the holding area. We will be keeping you and your party here, Captain. Your crew will undoubtedly prefer to cooperate with us if they understand you are hostages."

"Move that way," said Kelinda. "Keep together."

Their jail proved to be a cave, with a door constructed of some odd-looking transparent material, which Spock and Kirk were examining. Shea was also at the door, looking out, ostensibly watching Kelinda.

"I'm unable to determine the nature of the material, Captain," Spock said. "But I do not believe even phaser fire could disturb its molecular structure."

"All right, we can't break out. Maybe we can find another way."

"Captain," said Yeoman Thompson, "what do they want from us? What kind of people are they?"

"A good question, Yeoman."

"They registered as human," McCoy said.

"No, more than that, Doctor," Spock said, frowning. "They registered as *perfect* human life forms. I recall noting that the readings were almost textbook responses. Most curious."

"Spock," Kirk said, "what are the odds on such a parallel in life forms in another galaxy?"

"Based on those we have encountered in our own galaxy, the probability of humanoid development is high. But I would say the chances were very much against such an absolute duplication."

Shea turned slightly from the door. "Well, however perfect they are, sir, there don't seem to be very many of them."

"But they've got the paralysis field," Kirk said. "Rojan mentioned a central projector."

"If we can put it out of operation," McCoy said, "we've got a chance!"

"I am constrained to point out," said Spock, "that we do not even know what this projector looks like."

"No," Kirk said, "but those devices on their belts might indicate the position of the source."

"I would like to have one to examine."

"You'll have one, sir," Shea said. "If I have to rip one of the Kelvans apart to get it for you."

"Lieutenant Shea," Kirk said firmly, "you'll have your chance—but I'll tell you when."

"Yes, sir."

Kirk eyed him narrowly; but he could understand

the younger officer's defiant attitude toward their captors. "Spock, do you remember how you tricked that guard on Eminiar? The empathic mind touching—"

"Quite well, Captain. I made him think we had escaped."

"Can you do it again?"

"I will attempt it."

He checked Kelinda, who was standing fairly close to the bars, and then put his hands on the cave wall approximately behind her. Then he began to concentrate.

At first the Kelvan woman did not respond. Then she twitched a little, nervously, as though aware that something was wrong, but unable to imagine what. She glanced around, then straightened again.

Kirk signaled his people to position themselves along the wall, so that from outside the cave would appear to be empty. Then he bent and scooped some dirt from the loose, sandy floor.

Suddenly Spock broke out of his intense concentration, as though wrenched from it by something beyond him. He gasped and staggered back against the wall. At the same moment, Kelinda came to the door, opened it quickly and started in.

Kirk hurled his handful of dirt into her face. She cried out and clawed at her eyes. While she was half blinded, Kirk delivered a karate chop. It sent her sprawling, and, surprisingly, out. Kirk and McCoy dragged her the rest of the way inside.

"Mr. Spock—?"

"I . . . will be . . . quite all right, Captain. We must hurry."

"Bones, keep an eye on him. Let's go." He took the belt device from Kelinda and led the way out. He had hardly taken two steps before he was paralyzed again, the device dropping from his limp hands.

"I am sorry, Captain," said Rojan's voice. He came into view with Hanar, who went into the cave. "The escape attempt was futile. You cannot stop us and you cannot escape us."

Hanar reappeared. "Kelinda is somewhat bruised, Rojan, but otherwise unhurt."

Rojan nodded, and turning back to Kirk, released the party from the freeze. "I cannot let this go unpunished. This will serve as an example." He pointed to Yeoman Thompson and security chief Shea. "Hanar, take these two aside."

"What are you going to do?" McCoy said.

"This is not your affair, Doctor. Captain, as a leader, you realize the importance of discipline. I need you and these other specialists. But those two are unnecessary to me."

"You can't just kill them!" Kirk said.

Rojan did not respond. Thompson turned, looking pleadingly at Kirk. "Captain . . ."

"Rojan, let them go. I'm responsible for them."

"I think we are somewhat alike, Captain. Each of us cares less for his own safety than for the lives of his command. We feel pain when others suffer for our mistakes. Your punishment shall be to watch your people die."

Rojan touched his belt device. Shea and the girl seemed to vanish instantly. Where each of them had been standing was an odd geometrically shaped block, about the size of a fist.

Hanar picked them up and brought them to Rojan, who held them up to Kirk. "This is the essence of what those people were . . . The flesh and brain, and also what you call the personality, distilled down to these compact shapes. Once crushed—" He closed his hand over one, crushing it in his grip, letting the fragments sift through his fingers. "—they are no more. This person is dead. However—" He flipped the second block away. It bounced to a halt on the grass. Rojan again touched a button, and Shea was standing there, bewildered. "—this person can be restored. As I said, Captain—very practical."

They were herded back into the cave, leaving behind the fragments which were all that were left of a pretty girl.

Shocked and dispirited, they all sat down on the

cave floor but Shea. Spock's manner seemed more than usually distant.

"Mr. Spock," Kirk said, "are you sure you're all right?"

"Yes, quite all right, Captain."

McCoy said, "You looked very sick a while back, when you broke the mind lock."

"I did not break it," Spock said slowly. "I was ... shoved away by . . . something I have never experienced before."

"What was it?" said Kirk.

"Images ... bursting in my mind and consciousness. Colors ... shapes ... mathematical equations ... fused and blurred. I have been attempting to isolate them. So far, I have been able to recall clearly only one. Immense beings ... a hundred limbs that resemble tentacles, but are not ... minds of such control and capacity that each limb could do a different job."

"You mean," McCoy said, "that's what the Kelvans really are?"

"I do not know. It seemed the central image, but whether it was a source or a memory, I cannot tell."

"If they do normally look like that," Kirk said, "why did they adapt to bodies like ours?"

"For the sake of deception, what else?" McCoy said.

Kirk remembered the conversation they had overheard. "No, practicality. They chose the *Enterprise* as the best kind of vessel for the trip, and they need us to run her. We have to stay in our gravity and atmosphere, and they had to adapt to it ... We *have* to find a way to beat them. We outnumber them. Their only hold on us is the paralysis field."

"That's enough," said McCoy. "One wrong move and they jam all our neural circuits."

"Jamming," said Kirk. "That's it. Tricorders could analyze the frequency of the paralysis field. Spock, if you reverse the circuits on McCoy's neuroanalyzer, would it serve as a counterfield to jam the paralysis projector?"

"I am dubious about the possibility of success, Captain. The medical equipment is not built to put out any great amount of power. It would probably burn out."

"Is there any chance at all?"

"A small one."

"We'll take it. You and Bones have to get up to the ship."

"How?" said McCoy.

Kirk looked at his First Officer. "Spock, you're sick."

Spock's eyebrows went up. "Captain, I assure you that I am in excellent health."

"No, you're not. Dr. McCoy has examined you, and you're seriously ill. In fact, if he doesn't get you up to Sickbay you may die. And Rojan won't let that happen because he needs you to get through the barrier."

"It's a good idea," McCoy said, "but anybody looking at him can tell he's healthy."

"Vulcans have the ability to put themselves into a kind of trance . . . an enforced relaxation of every part of the mind and body. Right, Mr. Spock?"

"We find it more useful for resting the body than the so-called vacation."

"Can you do it now, and come out of it when you're in Sickbay? Say in half an hour?"

"It will take me a moment to prepare."

Shea walked to where he could watch for guards, then turned to nod and wave an all clear. Spock, remaining seated, composed himself very carefully. He seemed to be directing his attention inward upon himself. Then, almost as if someone had snapped off his switch, he flopped limply to one side.

McCoy rose to examine him, and at once looked a little alarmed. "Jim, his heartbeat really is way down—respiration almost nonexistent—"

Kirk turned to the door quickly and shouted "Guard! Guard!"

Hanar appeared. "What do you want, human?"

"Mr. Spock is ill. The doctor thinks he's dying."

"This illness came on him very suddenly," Hanar said. "Is it not unusual?"

"He's a Vulcan. They don't react like humans."

"Look, he may die," McCoy said as Hanar hesitated. "If I can get him up to Sickbay, there's a chance I can save him."

"Stand away from the door."

The others pulled away. Hanar came in, hand on his belt device, and bent to study the motionless Science Officer. He frowned. "I will have you beamed aboard, but you will be met by Tomar and watched."

As Hanar turned away, opening a communicator, Kirk and McCoy glanced toward each other.

"Do the best you can with him, Bones," Kirk said. McCoy nodded quickly, significantly.

The Kelvan Tomar and McCoy entered the *Enterprise's* examination room, supporting the limp Spock between them. Nurse Christine Chapel followed. "Doctor, what happened?"

McCoy ignored her. He said to Tomar, "Here. Put him down."

They eased Spock onto the table. Tomar peered curiously at the Vulcan, who was breathing only shallowly, and with alarmingly long pauses between breaths.

"Shall I summon more of your underlings?"

"I'll call my own underlings," McCoy said snappishly. "You stay out of the way. Miss Chapel, prepare two cc's of stokaline."

"Stokaline? But, Doctor—"

"Don't argue with me, Nurse. Get it."

Christine turned and went to get the required air hypo. McCoy activated the body function panel over the table and began to take readings, which were obviously low. Tomar hesitated, then moved away to where he could watch from a discreet distance.

Christine came back with the hypo, and at McCoy's nod, administered it, looking at her chief in puzzlement. There was no response from Spock for a moment. Then his eyes snapped open. McCoy shook his head very slightly and the eyes closed again. Over their heads, the readings began to pick up, some of them quickening, others returning to their Vulcan norms, which were almost surely strange to Tomar.

"This may be the turning point, Nurse. Prepare another shot."

"Doctor—"

"Miss Chapel, please follow orders."

She did so, though McCoy was well aware of her mounting puzzlement. He continued to study the panel. Finally he nodded. "That does it. He'll be all right now. Let him rest." He turned to Tomar. "It was a flare-up of Rigelian Kassaba fever. He suffered from it ten years ago, and it recurs now and then. There's no danger if he receives medication in time. He'll be up again in an hour or so."

"Very well. I will inform Rojan. You will stay here."

The Kelvan went out and McCoy went back to the table, grinning at Spock, who was now propped up on his elbows.

"I said I would awaken myself, Doctor. What was that shot you gave me?"

"It wasn't *a* shot. It was two."

"I am not interested in quantity, but in content."

"It was stokaline."

"I am not familiar with that drug. Are there any after effects?"

"Yes. You'll feel much better."

"It's a multiple vitamin compound," Christine said, beginning to look less confused.

McCoy patted Spock's shoulder. "Stop worrying. It'll put a little green in your cheeks. Let's get at the neuroanalyzer."

Spock grimaced and rolled off the table to his feet. "It would be helpful to have Mr. Scott here."

"Agreed. Miss Chapel, it is time for Mr. Scott's medical exam."

"I'll see that he reports immediately," Christine said demurely.

Hanar summoned Kirk out of the cave and brought him to Rojan, who was lounging comfortably by a lakeside, with Kelinda close by. Rojan waved Hanar away. "Proceed to the ship, Hanar. Rest yourself, Captain."

"What do you want with me now, Rojan?" Kirk said angrily.

"We will beam aboard the vessel shortly. I wish you to understand your duties."

"My duty is to stop you in any way I can."

"You will obey."

"Or you'll kill more of my people?"

"Captain, I cannot believe that you do not understand the importance of my mission," Rojan said slowly, as if trying to explain to an equal. "We Kelvans have a code of honor—harsh, demanding. It calls for much from us, and much from those we conquer. You have been conquered. I respect your devotion to your duty. But I cannot permit it to interfere with mine."

Kirk remained silent, thinking. It was impossible not to be impressed by what seemed to be so much straightforward honesty. It was apparent that that "code" was what Rojan lived by, and that he believed in it unshakably.

It was also impossible to forget the crumbled shards of what had been Yeoman Leslie Thompson, scattered in the grass not far from here.

Kelinda had moved away to a nearby burst of flowers. Rojan watched her, but not, Kirk thought, with any sign of ordinary male interest.

"I hunger to be in space again, Rojan," she said. "But these—these are lovely. Captain Kirk, what is it you call them?"

"Flowers," he said, moving closer to her, cautiously. "I don't know the variety."

"Our memory tapes tell us of such things on Kelva," Rojan said. "Crystals which form with such rapidity that they seem to grow. They look like these fragile things, somewhat. We call them 'sahsheer.'"

"The rose," Kirk said, "by any other name . . ."

"Captain?" Rojan said.

"A quotation, from a great human poet, Shakespeare. 'That which we call a rose by any other name would smell as sweet.'"

Kelinda bent to smell the flowers, while Kirk studied her. Did this woman in reality have a hundred tentacles, all adapted to different uses? It was hard to imagine.

"Kelinda, Captain, come away," Rojan said. "We must leave now."

Directly they were beamed up, Rojan directed Kirk to take him and Kelinda to the bridge. There, Uhura was at her station, and Chekov at his, but a Kelvan woman was in the Helmsman's seat, and Hanar was standing nearby.

"Drea has computed and laid a course for Kelva, Rojan," Hanar said.

"Sir," said Chekov, "we've jumped to warp eight."

"And we'll go faster yet," Rojan said. "Increase speed to warp eleven."

Chekov looked around sharply at Kirk, who could only shrug his helplessness and nod.

"On course and proceeding as planned," said the Kelvan woman at the helm, who was evidently Drea.

"Very well," said Rojan. "Hanar, proceed with the neutralizing operation."

Hanar nodded and went to the elevator. Kirk said quickly: "What neutralizing operation?"

"You humans are troublesome for us, Captain. There are not enough of us to effectively guard all of you all the time. Further, the food synthesizers cannot continue to manufacture food for all of you for our entire journey. We are therefore neutralizing all nonessential personnel."

"No!"

"Captain, you can do nothing to stop it. The procedure is already under way. Now, as to bridge personnel . . ." He moved toward Uhura. "We have no need of communications for some centuries."

Uhura sat frozen in her chair, staring at Rojan in horror. He touched his belt device—and there was nothing left in her seat but a geometrical solid.

"And since Drea is now capable of doing our navigating—" Chekov too vanished. Drea had already neutralized two crewmen beyond Scott's station. Kirk stood frozen.

"They are not dead, Captain," Rojan reminded him. "They are merely reduced to the sum total of what they are."

"That's very comforting," Kirk said sarcastically. "But not pleasant to watch. I'm going to Sickbay. My First Officer was taken ill."

"Yes, I was informed. Go ahead."

Sickbay was deserted. Kirk found Scott, McCoy and Spock picking at food at a table in the recreation room. Getting himself a tray, he joined them. "Reports, gentlemen?"

"I'm a little sick," McCoy said. "We burned out my neuroanalyzer, to no effect. I saw one of the Kelvans, the one they call Tomar, reduce four of my doctors and nurses to those . . . little blocks."

"I've seen them do that too. Remember, the process is reversible. I only wonder how far it's going to go."

"I have been checking our table of organization against their apparent capabilities," Spock said. "It appears that we will have very few 'survivors.' They will need none of the security men, for example. And once we cross the energy barrier, Engineering can be reduced to a skeleton crew. Beyond that point lies some three hundred years of straight cruising—at an astonishing velocity, to be sure, but still cruising. And of the officers, it would seem that only we four could be regarded as 'essential.' I am not even sure of your status, Captain, or mine."

"How so?"

"Rojan is in command now."

"Quite so," Kirk said bitterly. "Scotty, have you found out anything about the paralysis projector?"

"Quite a lot, and none of it good. The machine is in Engineering, and it's encased in that same stuff the door of our jail was made of. Furthermore, it's nae a simple machine—and it's the only one of its kind on board. I think it must be the source of all their special powers—and it's impregnable."

"Any suggestions?"

"One," Scott said. "Self-destruct."

Kirk considered it. "We've been driven to that point, or almost, once before," he said at last. "But aside from my aversion to suicide—and the deaths of everybody else—it's not practicable. We'd never complete the routine with the computer before Rojan paralyzed us."

"I thought of that," Scott said. "I could do it myself, though. Remember that we've got to cross the energy barrier. It willna be easy at best. A little sabotage in the matter-antimatter nacelles, and we'd blow, for good and all."

Kirk made a quick silencing gesture. Tomar had come in, and was now approaching them, staring curiously at their trays.

"I do not understand," he said, "why you go to the trouble of consuming this bulk material to sustain yourselves." He pulled a flat pillbox from a pocket and opened it. "These contain all the required nutritional elements."

"Not for human forms," McCoy said. "Bulk is necessary to our digestive systems, and there's a limit to the amount of energy that can be crammed into a pill, too. Perhaps you haven't been in human form long enough to find just pills debilitating, but you will—you will."

"Indeed? Then you had better show me promptly what else we shall need, and how to manage it."

McCoy looked rebellious and Kirk himself felt a hope die almost before it had been born. "I think you'd better, Bones," he said.

"All right. Come on, I'll show you how to work the selector." McCoy led Tomar off toward the wall dispenser.

"Spock," Kirk said in a whisper, "shall we self-destruct? Crossing the barrier may be our last chance to do so."

"Granted," Spock whispered back. "But it is said on Earth that while there is life, there is hope. That is sound logic: no multivalued problem has only one solution."

"Well, we couldn't knock out their central machine even if we were able. It has to be kept intact to restore the rest of our people to human form."

There was quite a long silence. McCoy had settled Tomar at a table with a tray, and Tomar was gingerly forking some meat into his mouth. Judging by his nod, he found it agreeable, and he began eating at a fair speed for a newcomer to the habit. McCoy grinned and rejoined his colleagues.

"I'm almost sorry I did that," he said. "It looks like he likes food—and I wouldn't want any of them to enjoy anything."

Spock continued to watch Tomar. "Most peculiar."

"What is?" Kirk said.

"The isolated glimpses of things I saw when I touched Kelinda's mind are beginning to coalesce in my consciousness. The Kelvans have superior intellectual capacity. But to gain it, they apparently sacrificed many things that would tend to distract them. Among these are the pleasures of the senses—and, of course, emotions."

"But then, Tomar shouldn't be enjoying the taste of food."

"He has taken human form," Spock said, "and is having human reactions."

Kirk's mind leapt ahead in response. "If they all respond to stimulation of the senses, maybe we could confuse them. They don't know how to handle those senses yet. If we can distract them enough, we could try to get the belt devices away. That's their only hold on us."

"It seems reasonable," Spock said.

"All right. We watch for opportunities to work on them—hit them every way we can think of."

Scott was studying Tomar. "I can think of one way right off," he said. He rose and went to the Kelvan. "Lad, you'll be needing something to wash that down with. Have you ever tried Saurian brandy?"

McCoy stopped Hanar as the Kelvan was passing by the door to the examination room. "Come on in a moment, please, Hanar."

"What is it, human?"

"I've noticed you're not looking too well."

"Impossible. We do not malfunction, as do you humans."

"No? You're forgetting you're in a human body. And that does malfunction—that's why Rojan considers me essential. You look pale." He gestured to the table. "Sit up there."

When Hanar complied, McCoy picked up his medical tricorder and began taking readings. "Uh huh . . . Hmmm . . . I don't know about that . . . Hmmmm."

"Please articulate, human."

"Well, it looks to me like this body of yours is getting a little anemic, and has some other subclinical deficiencies. Comes from taking your food in pills, instead of good solid substance." He turned aside and picked up a hypo, which he set.

"What are you doing?"

"I'm going to give you a shot—high potency vitamin-mineral concentrate. You'll have to have one three times a day for a few days. And eat some solid food."

It had taken Scott a while to get Tomar down to serious drinking; initially he had been too interested in the tartan, the claymore, the armorial bearings on the walls, the standing suit of ancient armor in Scott's quarters, all of which he declared nonfunctional in a starship. He did not seem to grasp either the concept of mementos or that of decoration.

Finally, however, they were seated at Scott's desk with a bottle and glasses between them. After a while, it was two bottles. Tomar seemed to remain in total control of himself, as if he'd been drinking lemonade. "No more?" he said.

"Well . . . no more Saurian brandy, but . . ." Scott looked around and found another bottle. "Now, y'see, this liquor is famous on Ahbloron—I mean, Aldibibble—on one of these planets we go to."

"It is a different color from the other."

"Yes. And stronger, too." He poured some into Tomar's glass with an unsteady hand, and then, perforce, some into his own. Somehow this experiment was not working out right.

Kirk paid a call on the cabin Kelinda had commandeered. When she invited him in, he found her looking at a tape on a viewscreen. "Did I disturb you?"

"Disturb? What is it you wish?"

He went over to her. "I want to apologize."

"I do not understand, Captain."

"For hitting you. I wanted to say I was sorry."

"That is not necessary. You attempted to escape, as we would have. That I was taken in by your ruse is my fault, not yours."

Kirk smiled and reached out to touch her face gently. "I don't usually hit beautiful women."

"Why not, if there is need?"

"Because there are better things for men and women to do." He moved the hand down to her neck. "Was it here that I hit you?"

"No, on the other side."

"Oh." He leaned to the other side, kissed her neck, and nuzzled her ear. "Is that better?"

"Better? Was it intended to be a remedy?"

"This is." Drawing her to her feet, he took her in his arms and kissed her.

After a moment she drew back. "Is there some significance to this action?"

"It was meant to express . . . well, among humans it shows warmth, love—"

"Oh. You are trying to seduce me," she said, as if she were reading a weather report. "I have been reading about you."

"Me?"

"Humans. This business of love. You have devoted much literature to it. Why have you built such a mystique around a simple biological fact?"

"We enjoy it."

"The literature?"

"Kelinda, I'm sorry I brought the subject up."

"Did you regard this contact of the lips as pleasurable?"

Kirk sighed. "I did."

"Curious. I wonder why." Abruptly she put her arms around him and kissed him back.

The door opened and Rojan came in. Kirk made a point of drawing back with guilty swiftness.

"Is there some problem, Captain?" Rojan said.

"None." Kirk left quickly. Rojan stared after him.

"What did he want here?"

"He came to apologize for hitting me," Kelinda said. "Apparently, it involves some peculiar touching contacts."

"In what manner?"

Kelinda hesitated, then reached up to nibble at Rojan's neck and ear. Rojan stepped away from her, frowning.

"They are odd creatures, these humans. Please have the reports on fuel consumption relayed to Subcommander Hanar as soon as possible."

Spock had taught Rojan to play chess; the Kelvan had learned with breathtaking speed. They were playing now, in the recreation room.

"Yes, they are peculiar," Spock said, moving a piece. "I very often find them unfathomable, but an interesting psychological study."

Rojan moved in return. "I do not understand this business of biting someone's neck to apologize."

Spock looked up, raising his eyebrows. Then he looked back at the game, saw an opening and quickly moved another piece. "I believe you are referring to a kiss. But it is my understanding that such, uh, apologies are usually exchanged between two people who have some affection for each other."

"Kelinda has no affection for Captain Kirk," Rojan said quickly.

Spock studied Rojan's next move and shook his

head. "You seemed disturbed about the incident. Your game is off."

"Why should I be disturbed?"

"It seems to me you have known Kelinda for some time. She is a Kelvan, as you are. Among humans, I have found the symptoms you are displaying would be indicative of jealousy."

"I have no reason for such a reaction. Kelinda is a female. Nothing more."

"Captain Kirk seems to find her quite attractive."

"Of course she is."

"But you are not jealous."

"No!"

"Nor upset."

"Certainly not!"

Spock made his move. "Checkmate."

Kirk, Spock and McCoy were holding another council of war in the recreation room. Kirk was depressed. "The thing is, I can't tell if we're getting anywhere. And I haven't seen Scotty for what seems like months."

"You haven't seen Tomar either," McCoy said. "But the point is, these things take time. The Kelvans started out with adapted human bodies in superb physical shape—textbook cases, as Spock said. They have high resistance. I've been giving Hanar shots that would have driven our whole crew up the wall in an hour. He responds slowly—but he's getting more irritable by the minute, now."

"And Rojan," Spock said, "has exhibited symptoms of jealousy toward Kelinda and you."

"What about Kelinda, Jim?" McCoy said.

"No progress," Kirk said, uncomfortably.

"What approach did you take with her? Could be you're a little rusty—"

Kirk felt himself begin to bristle. Spock interposed smoothly: "I would say it is sufficient that Rojan is jealous."

"Right," Kirk said quickly. "That's the opening wedge. As soon as it's a little wider, we move."

Behind Kirk, Kelinda's voice said: "I would like to speak with you, Captain."

Spock stood up at once. "Doctor, I think I need another dose of stokaline."

"Huh?" McCoy said. "Oh, yes. Pardon us."

They went out. Kirk leaned back in his chair and studied Kelinda. "You had something to say?"

"Yes." Did she really seem a trifle uncomfortable, even perhaps awkward? Kirk waited. Then she took a deep breath and touched him, lightly, on a shoulder. "This cultural mystique surrounding a biological function . . ."

"Yes?"

"You realize it really is quite overdone."

"Oh. Quite."

"However, I was wondering . . . would you please apologize to me again?"

Rojan was in the command chair. Behind him, the elevator doors snapped open, and then Hanar's voice said, with surprising belligerence: "Rojan. I want to talk to you."

Rojan looked up in surprise. "Very well, Hanar."

"First, I do not like the way responsibility and duty have been portioned out to us."

"It is the way your duties have always been assigned."

"And that is my second quarrel with you. It was always unjust—"

Rojan snapped out of the chair. "Hanar—"

"And further, I do not care much for the autocratic way you order us about on this ship, which we captured, not you—"

"Confine yourself to your quarters!"

Hanar hesitated, as though he had had a lot more to say, but had thought better of it. Then he spun on his heel and left without further acknowledgment.

Rojan found his own fists clenching in anger—and was suddenly aware that Drea was watching him in amazement from the navigator's station. As Rojan turned his back to hide his expression, Spock came onto the bridge and went toward his library-computer. Rojan followed.

"You were not called to the bridge, Spock. What is your purpose here?"

"Sensors and various other recording devices require monitoring and certain adjustments."

"Very well, proceed . . . Have you seen Captain Kirk?"

"Do you want him? I will call him to the bridge."

"No. I . . . wondered where he was."

"Dr. McCoy and I left him some time ago in the recreation room."

"He was alone, then?"

"No. Kelinda was with him. She seemed most anxious to speak to him."

"I told him to stay away from her."

"It would appear that you have little control over her, sir . . . or perhaps Captain Kirk has more."

Rojan turned abruptly and headed for the elevator.

Kirk and Kelinda were locked in a kiss when Rojan came through the recreation room door. Kirk looked up, but did not release Kelinda entirely; instead he kept a possessive arm around her as he turned toward Rojan. Rojan stopped and stared.

"Kelinda, I told you to avoid this human!"

"I did not wish to," she said.

"I am your commander."

"I've found," Kirk said, "that doesn't mean much to a woman if she's bound to go her own way."

"You have done this to her! Corrupted her—turned her away from me!"

"If you couldn't keep her, Rojan, that's not *my* problem."

Furiously, Rojan leaped at Kirk. He seemed to have forgotten all about the belt device, his bare hands reaching out. Kirk pushed Kelinda aside and met Rojan's rush.

The two men, equally powerful, slammed at each other like bulls. Rojan was more clumsy, more unaccustomed to the body he was in. Kirk was the quicker and the more adept fighter, but he was not possessed by the anger which obviously drove Rojan.

Kelinda did not intervene; she only watched. After a moment she was joined by Spock and McCoy.

Kirk delivered a final punch that sent Rojan spinning down, backward. But he was not beaten yet. He started to climb back to his feet.

"Rojan—wait!" Kirk said. "Listen to me—"

Rojan flung himself forward, but Kirk fended him off. "Listen! Why didn't you use your paralyzer? Don't you know why? Because you've become a human yourself." Kirk ducked a punch. "Look at you—brawling like a street fighter—shaking with rage—"

Rojan paused and stared as the words began to sink in. "What?"

"You thought I took your woman away from you. You were jealous—and you wanted to kill me with your bare hands. Would a Kelvan have done that? Would he *have* to? You reacted with the emotions of a human, Rojan. You are one."

"No! We cannot be."

"You have no choice. You chose this ship. Because of its environmental systems, you had to take human form to use it. And you're stuck with it—you and your descendants—for the next three hundred years. Look what's happened to you in the short time you've been exposed to us. What do you think will happen in three hundred years? When this ship gets to Kelva, the people on it will be aliens, the Kelvans their enemies.

"We have a mission. We must carry it out." But Rojan's tone showed that he was shaken.

"Your mission was to find worlds for your people to live on. You can still do that. I told you we could present your case to the Federation. I know it would be sympathetic. There are many unpopulated planets in our galaxy. You could develop them in peace, your way."

"They would do that? You would extend welcome to invaders?"

"No. But we do welcome friends."

"Perhaps," said Rojan, "perhaps it could be done."

Spock said: "A robot ship could be sent back to Kelva with the Federation proposal."

"But what of us?" Rojan said. "If we . . . if we retain this form, where can we find a place?"

"Seems to me," McCoy said, "that little planet you were on was kind of a nice place."

"Pleasant . . . but . . ."

"The Federation would probably grant a colonization permit to a small group of people who desired to settle there," Spock said. "You do represent an old and highly intelligent race."

Rojan turned to Kelinda and jerked his head at Kirk. "You would want to go with him?"

Kelinda glanced at Kirk and then back at Rojan. "As you have said, he is not our kind. I believe I owe you an apology." She kissed him. "It *is* pleasurable, Rojan."

"You know, Rojan," Kirk said, "one of the advantages of being a human is being able to appreciate beauty . . . of a flower, or of a woman. Unless you'd rather conquer a galaxy?"

"No, Captain, I would rather not." Rojan took Kelinda's hand. "A link in a chain—that's all we were. Perhaps there is an opportunity for us to be more." He turned away, crossed the room and activated an intercom. "Bridge, this is Rojan."

"Yes, Commander," said Drea's voice.

"Turn the ship. We are returning to the alien . . . We are returning home."

"Sir?"

"Turn the ship about."

He led Kelinda out. Kirk, Spock and McCoy expelled simultaneous sighs of relief.

"Jim, I was coming to tell you—"

"Yes, Bones?"

"I found Scotty in his room with Tomar. Apparently they've been having a drinking bout all this time. They were both under the table—but Tomar went down first. Scott had Tomar's belt device in his hand. He just never made it to the door with it."

Kirk grinned. "The Kelvans," he said, "still have a lot to learn about being human, don't they?"

THE CLOUD MINDERS

(Margaret Armen, David Gerrold and Oliver Crawford)

"Then there's been a mistake," Kirk said.

And he couldn't afford one, not on this mission. During a routine check of the *Enterprise*'s operational quadrant of the galaxy, they had been ordered by the Federation to make top warp speed to the planet Ardana, sole source of a trace metal able to arrest a botanical plague ravaging vegetation which made a neighboring planet habitable. It was a mission whose emergency nature was known to the High Advisor of Ardana. Yet his greeting to the *Enterprise* had contained no reference to the zenite mines. Instead, his welcome specified Stratos as the reception site.

"Stratos is their Cloud City, isn't it, Mr. Spock?"

"It is, Captain."

Kirk hit the intercom to the Transporter Room. "Mr. Scott, are you locked in on the mines of Ardana or its Cloud City?"

"The mines, Captain. That's what you ordered."

Then this mistake isn't ours, Kirk thought. The Ardanans understood the Transporter; they had it themselves. Turning to Uhura, he said tersely, "Tell the High Advisor we request that the official welcoming courtesies be dispensed with. We are beaming down directly to the mines to ensure the fastest possible transport of the zenite to Marak II. The need is desperate. Say we appreciate the honor and look forward to a visit to Cloud City in the future ... Come with me, Mr. Spock."

But no miners were awaiting them at the mine-shaft entrance. The hill by which they'd arrived was deserted.

"I don't understand it," Kirk said. "The Troglyte miners were to make delivery when we beamed down."

"Perhaps there is another entrance," Spock suggested.

There was none. The other side of the hill was as abandoned, as bleak and forbidding as the rest of their arrival area. It was Spock who put the thought in both of their minds into words. "It would seem that the Troglytes have changed their minds about the delivery, sir."

Even as Kirk nodded there came a hiss in the air above their heads. Two heavy, noosed thongs were hurled from behind them with an accuracy that pinned their arms helplessly to their bodies. Jerks tightened the thongs, and the two *Enterprise* officers were pulled roughly around to confront four creatures, obvious Troglytes, their loose miners' overalls begrimed, their eyes begoggled, their features hidden by slitted masks. One of the Troglytes was slightly smaller than the others; but they all had long, sharp-edged mortae, the honed blades aimed in open threat.

"What is the reason for this attack?" Kirk demanded.

"Interference breeds attack," the smallest Troglyte said coldly, in a female voice. "My name is Vanna, Captain. I have need of your ... services. Move on." The overalled arm motioned to the mine-shaft entrance.

"We are here by permission of your government Council," Kirk said. "On emergency mission."

"Move on, Captain." Ominous ice entered the voice.

Kirk felt the prod of her sharp blade in his back. Exchanging a swift glance with Spock, they burst into simultaneous action, lashing out with their feet at the two nearest Troglytes. Spock's kick caught his man in the chest. It felled him just as Kirk's foot, slamming into his captor's stomach, dropped him to the ground, knocking the wind out of him.

Vanna lunged at Kirk, but he had broken clear of his bonds and knocked her weapon out of her hand. Spock and the remining Troglyte circled each other warily. Vanna, agile and swift, lunged at Kirk with her bare hands and they fell to the ground. In the struggle, the strap securing her goggles snapped. They slipped from her face to reveal feminine features of such surprising beauty that Kirk, lost in amazement, had no eyes for what was materializing on the Transporter coordinates.

It was her wince at the sudden glare of sunlight that brought him out of his trance. A man of patrician bearing stood behind them. He wore a togalike garment and the charismatic air of the born ruler. Two husky males, armed and uniformed in gleaming white, shimmered into sight beside him—guards.

The patrician spoke. "Troglytes! Halt!"

He was not obeyed. Vanna, unyielding, continued to writhe in Kirk's grasp. Spock was now trying to cope with two of the miners, as the third elbowed groggily from the ground where the Vulcan's first kick had landed him.

"Surrender—or we'll fire!"

Wrenching an arm free, Vanna tried to rake Kirk's face with her nails. He pulled back slightly, and seizing her chance to break his hold, she leaped to her feet and ran to the mine entrance, shouting to her companions. They joined her, racing after her amid a shower of shining pellets. One of the missiles from the guards' guns struck. Zigzagging, hunkered low, the three unwounded Troglytes disappeared into the mine entrance.

Kirk, climbing slowly to his feet, was frowning in preoccupation, his eyes following Vanna and her vanished companions. Spock stooped to retrieve the communicator which had dropped from his belt, and straightened to meet the approach of their rescuers.

"Are you harmed, gentlemen?" asked the toga-clad man.

"Just a little shaken up," Kirk said.

"I am Plasus, High Advisor for the planet Council."

Kirk acknowledged the introduction briefly. "Captain Kirk, *Enterprise*. My First Officer, Mr. Spock."

"My regrets for the unpleasantness of your welcome to Ardana, gentlemen."

"It was rather warm," Kirk said dryly.

"Unfortunately, violence is habitual with the Troglytes. I can assure you, Captain, this insult will not go unpunished."

It was Spock's turn to frown in thought as Kirk said, "I am more concerned with that zenite consignment. Why isn't it in its specified location?"

Urbane, unruffled, the High Advisor's face with its high-bridged nose assumed a look of sadness. "Apparently the Disruptors have confiscated it, as I feared they would. They're a small group of Troglyte malcontents who hold the others under complete domination. It is the Disruptors who are responsible for the others' refusal to continue mining zenite."

"But they agreed to this delivery," Kirk protested. "It was your Council which assured us of that."

Plasus nodded benignly. "Obviously," he said, "they agreed as a ruse to get valuable hostages."

"Hostages? For what purpose?"

"To force the Council to meet their demands." Plasus turned to his guards. "Pick up the injured Troglyte for later questioning . . . Then organize a search party for the zenite consignment." Once more the urbane host, he said to Kirk, "Meanwhile, Captain, I suggest that you and First Officer Spock be our guests in Stratos City."

"I hope the search will be brief," Kirk said.

A shadow of grimness darkened the urbanity for a

fleeting second. "I assure you we will do everything in our power to make it so. Now if you will just step this way, over here, our own Transporter will pick us all up."

They were led into a large, oddly designed chamber. Its floor and three of its walls glittered with a subdued iridescence. The fourth wall had been left open to the expanse of sky beyond, its border a waist-high balustrade of the same iridescent material. There was a careful carelessness about the manner in which luxuriously cushioned benches were scattered about the room, a calculated casualness that matched the surrealistic sculptural forms which decorated it. Central to it was a small dais, flanked by two straggly carved poles of almost ceiling height. They struck Kirk as purposeless even as decoration.

From the balustrade, Spock called, "Captain, here, sir, please!"

The whole planet was spread out beneath them. Its surface could be only half seen through drifting mists. What was visible was dwarfed by distance to the dimensions of a relief map, its hills anonymous mounds, its valleys vague shadows. There was both beauty and terror in such eminence. It evoked a feeling of uneasiness in Kirk.

"Remarkable," Spock said. "The finest example of sustained antigravity elevation I have ever seen."

The sound of a door opening behind them made them turn. A young woman had entered the room of antigravity triumph. She was tall, willow-slim, willow-graceful, her golden hair a mist of mystery around her perfect face. She didn't walk—she glided, her approaching movement so supple it lacked all suggestion of bone or skeletal muscle. Like the clouds which obscured the planet's contours, she drifted toward the two *Enterprise* officers.

"My father," she said to Plasus, "your sentinels informed me of our honored guests' arrival. I came to extend my greetings."

"Gentlemen, my daughter—one of our planet's

incomparable works of art. Droxine, Captain James Kirk and his First Officer, Mr. Spock."

Her eyes lingered for a moment on the satyr ears of the First Officer. "I have never met a Vulcan before, sir," she said demurely.

Spock bowed. "Nor I a work of art, madame."

Kirk looked at Spock with quizzical amusement and surprise. Plasus beckoned his guests back into the room from the balcony. "Come, gentlemen, there is much to see in our city. This is our Council gallery. We have some of our finest art forms assembled here for the viewing of all our city dwellers. That piece there can boast of a special—"

He stopped abruptly. The piece he had turned to was a transparent solid of flowing serpentine lines curled like coiling flames. A miner's mortae had been driven into it, webbing it with cracks.

"Disruptors again!" Furiously, Plasus jerked the tool from the sculpture and dashed it to the floor.

"They are despoiling the whole city," Droxine said.

"For what purpose?" Spock asked.

"Again, to force the Council to accede to their demands." Plasus spoke with the impatience of an adult irritated by a half-witted child.

"Just what are these demands?" Kirk said.

"Nothing you need concern yourself about, Captain."

Kirk's voice was very quiet. "I must concern myself with anything that interferes with the delivery of the zenite, Mr. Advisor."

"Mr. Advisor, plant life is the source of oxygen," Spock added. "If all plant life is destroyed on Marak II, all humanoid and animal life will end there with it."

Plasus had recovered his suavity. "I assure you, gentlemen, you will get what you came for."

"I hope so," Kirk said. He paused. "Ardana is a member of the Federation. It is your Council's responsibility that nothing interferes with its obligation to another Federation member."

"And we accept the responsibility."

Spock touched the webbed cracks in the sculpture. "But why destroy art forms? They are a loss to everybody."

"Art means nothing to the Disruptors." Plasus stooped to pick up the mortae. "*This* is the only form they understand." Rage overpowered him again. Nobody spoke as he fought to regain control of himself. "But no doubt you would like to rest. A chamber has been prepared for you. Sentinels will conduct you to it, gentlemen."

It was dismissal. Droxine's eyes followed Spock as the two from the *Enterprise* left the room.

"The Disruptors must be mad," she said, "to have attacked two such charming strangers."

"They grow more daring every day," Plasus said.

"Do you think the Captain and his very attractive officer will feel we are responsible?"

Plasus smiled indulgently down on his daughter. "Responsible for injuries done to the charming strangers—or to our diplomatic ties?"

Droxine flushed. "Oh, I was concerned about both, father."

Plasus laughed outright. "I am sure they will not blame you."

She exhaled a breath of relief. "I'm glad. I like them. They are not at all like our men of Ardana ... Father, promise me not to find the zenite too soon?"

Before he could reply, two guards burst into the room. Between them was a powerful man, his muscular shoulders tensed against their grip, but not struggling to free himself. That he had been doing so before was evident in the guards' panting.

"Apologies, Mr. Advisor," said one of them. "This Troglyte was apprehended leaving the city. As he lacks a transport card, we thought you would want to question him."

The man's aspect bore little resemblance to the stunted figures of other Troglytes. Despite the grime of his miner's overalls, the unkempt tangle of his shoulder-length hair, he was handsome. Proudly he drew himself to his full height, his eyes bright with scorn as they fixed on Plasus.

"What is your business in Stratos City, Troglyte?" demanded the High Advisor.

Though the flashing eyes burned with hate, the lips were silent.

"Speak! I command you!"

"My business is to repair," said the prisoner.

"Indeed. Then you must have a repair order. Where is it?"

"It was forgotten."

"Did you also forget your transport card?" The question was harsh with irony.

"It was lost when your sentinels attacked me."

"And where was your cavern mortae lost?" Plasus pointed to the empty sheath at the waist of the overalls. Then, striding to the mutilated sculpture, he plunged the mortae he still held in his hand into the hole it had made. "Here, perhaps."

"I came to make repairs," the prisoner said stubbornly.

"You shall make them—by telling me the names of the Disruptors."

"I know nothing."

"I would advise you to increase your knowledge."

An open sneer distorted the handsome face. "That is not possible for a Troglyte. The Stratos City dwellers have said so."

"Secure him to the dais," Plasus told the guards.

They tried to. But as they pushed the miner toward the dais, he knocked one guard aside and raced for the iridescent balustrade. The guards moved for their guns, but Plasus shouted, "*No!* I want him alive!"

It was too late. The prisoner had flung himself over the balustrade.

After a moment, Plasus shrugged. "How unfortunate," he said philosophically. "How unfortunate." He went out.

Droxine, as composed as her father, had been busying herself with an arrangement of goblets on a cubical table. The gold metal of one rang as she set it down, and a moment later, Spock came through the still open doors of the Council chamber.

"Mr. Spock!" the girl cried. "I thought you had accompanied Captain Kirk to the rest chamber down the corridor."

"There was some disturbance," the First Officer said. "It awakened me."

"I was but setting the table. I did not realize I would disturb you."

"Only Vulcan ears would find such a noise discernible from such a distance," Spock said.

The perfect eyelids lifted. "It seems Vulcans are fascinatingly different," said their owner. "In many ways."

Their eyes met. "The same may be said of inhabitants of Stratos," Spock observed.

"Vulcan eyes seem to be very discerning, too." She drew him down on the bench beside her.

His attention was sufficiently on this Ardanan work of art for him to fail his reputation for discerning sight for once. Behind him, a small figure draped in the clothing of Stratos crept from behind a pillar and moved stealthily down the corridor.

In the rest chamber, Kirk, breathing evenly, lay apparently asleep on a wide, billowy-pillowed dais. Vanna, crossing to him silently, drew a mortae from under her gown and laid its blade against his throat.

Kirk opened his eyes and he seized Vanna's wrist. Twisting the mortae from her grasp, he fell back with her on the bed. She kicked and writhed, but shortly he got her arms pinned back above her head.

"Well, that's better," he said, breathing evenly. "You again!" The face beneath his chest was lovelier than he remembered; but its eyes were cold as death.

"You sleep lightly, Captain," Vanna said.

"And I see you've changed your dressmaker."

"Release me," she said tonelessly.

"So you can attack me again?"

"Then call the guards," she told him contemptuously. "They will protect you."

"But I don't want protection. I find this very enjoyable."

"I do not."

Kirk grinned down at her. "All right, I'll make a bargain with you. Answer some questions, and I'll let you up."

"What questions?"

Kirk shook his head. "First, your word."

Hesitation came and went in her face. "I will answer."

Kirk released her. Panther-swift, she leaped to her feet and stooped for the mortae beside the bed. As he gripped her wrist again, he became aware that Spock's bed was empty. Where *was* Spock in this place of sudden treacheries? With that gliding girl?

The gliding girl was leaning back against a down cushion, its cream less creamy than the skin of her face. Spock, sitting very erect, was saying, "Yes, we Vulcans pride ourselves on our logic."

"Also on complete control of your emotions?"

"Emotions interfere with logic," he said firmly.

"Is that why you take mates only once in seven years?"

"The seven-year cycle is biological. At that time the mating drive outweighs all other motivation."

Droxine moved her head from the pillow and rested it against his shoulder. He looked down at the spindrift of golden hair, its fragrance in his nostrils, and their eyes locked. "Can nothing disturb the cycle, Mr. Spock?"

The Vulcan logician cleared his throat. "Exceptional feminine beauty is always disturbing, madame."

She had lifted her mouth toward his when a clang resounded from down the corridor. Spock sprang from the bench and ran for the door. Rushing into the rest chamber, he stopped dead at the sight of Vanna. Kirk had wrenched the mortae from her once more and dashed it to the floor.

"Captain, are you all right?"

From behind him Droxine cried, "*Vanna!* Why have you come here?"

Disheveled but still proud in her disarray, the Troglyte girl bent in a low bow to Kirk and Spock. "To welcome our honored guests," she said in a voice that cut with sarcasm. "Just as I was taught to do when I served in your father's household."

"It seems the Troglytes have the impression that our ship is here to intimidate them," Kirk told Spock.

"It is not an impression, Captain," Vanna said hotly. "It is truth!"

Kirk picked up her mortae and shoved it into his belt. "We are here to get that consignment of zenite. Nothing more."

"Starships do not transport cargo!" Vanna cried.

"In times of emergency they do anything," Kirk said. "And believe me, this plant plague on Marak II is an extreme emergency."

"Lies will not keep the Troglytes in their caverns, and neither will your ship, Captain."

Droxine said, "You speak like a Disruptor, Vanna."

"I speak for my people! They have as much right to the skies as you Stratos dwellers!"

"What would Troglytes do here?" asked Droxine disdainfully.

"Live! With warmth and light as everyone should!"

"Your caverns are warm," said Droxine coldly. "And your eyes are unaccustomed to light. Just as your minds are unaccustomed to reason." She moved to a wall and pressed a button. A sentinel appeared at the door; and waving a casual hand toward Vanna, Droxine said, "Take her away."

Kirk looked at Spock. "Surely," he said to Droxine, "you don't deny light and warmth to the Troglytes?"

"The Troglytes are workers," said the child of the High Advisor. "They mind zenite and till the soil. Those things can't be done here."

"In other words," Spock said, "they perform all the physical toil necessary to maintain Stratos?"

Droxine smiled at him. "That is their function in our society."

"Yet they are not allowed to share its advantages?"

"How can they share what they don't understand?"

"They could be taught to understand," Kirk said.

Droxine's answer had the sound of a lesson learned by rote. "The complete separation of toil and leisure has given Ardana a perfectly balanced social system."

Kirk was finding this conversation increasingly disturbing. He began to pace. Spock said, " 'Troglyte' is a corruption of an ancient Earth term, Captain. Its technical translation is 'cave dweller.' "

Kirk threw him a tight nod. "We should have realized—"

He was interrupted by a shriek of agony echoing from the Council gallery. He and Spock exchanged a glance of alarm and raced down the corridor to the room of luxuriously cushioned benches.

Tied tightly to its central dais, Vanna was screaming. Incandescing rays from its flanking poles flooded her face with green fire. She shrieked again.

Droxine went back to the cubical table and straightened a gold goblet, while Plasus watched. Kirk and Spock sprang to the dais to tear at the cords that bound Vanna's writhings.

"Stop it!" Kirk shouted at Plasus. There was a long moment. Then Plasus' hands came together in a faint clap. The rays faded. Still bound, Vanna slumped into unconsciousness.

"She is stubborn," Plasus said. "Physical discomfort is the only persuasion they understand, Captain."

"You have tortured her." Kirk's voice shook with anger.

"Is it preferable to spare Vanna—and allow an entire planet to be destroyed? You yourself pointed out that the search for your zenite must be short." Plasus' voice was eminently reasonable.

Spock approached Droxine. "Violence in reality is quite different from theory. Do you not agree, madame?"

"But nothing else moves the Troglytes. What else can they understand?"

"All those little things you and I understand," the

Vulcan said gravely. "Such as kindness, justice, equality."

She shivered slightly. Then she drew a fold of her gown around her, rose gracefully and left the gallery.

"The abstract concepts of an intellectual society are beyond the comprehension of the Troglytes, Mr. Spock." The High Advisor was angry now.

"The abstract concept of loyalty seems clear to Vanna," Kirk said.

"A few Troglytes are brought here as retainers. Vanna was one of them. They receive more training than the others."

"But obviously no more consideration," Kirk said.

Open rage thickened Plasus' voice. "I fail to see the use of this continued criticism." He beckoned to his guards and pointed to the slumped body on the dais. "Revive her!"

Kirk leaped to the dais. "The only way you'll use that device again is on both of us!"

"An imposing display of primitive gallantry, Captain. You realize, of course, that I can have my guards remove you."

"Of course," Kirk said. "But Starfleet Command seldom takes kindly to having either rays or physical force used on one of its personnel. Think twice."

Plasus did so. "Why are you so concerned about this Disruptor's well-being, Captain Kirk?"

"I want that zenite."

"Then stop interfering—and I'll get it for you. We will get it for you in our own way. Guards, take the prisoner to confinement quarters. As for you, Captain, you will return to your starship at once—or I shall contact your Starfleet Command myself to report your interference in this planet's society, in contravention of your prime directive. Should you reappear on Stratos City again, it would be only as an enemy."

The guards were removing Vanna's unconscious body from the dais. Kirk clicked open his communicator.

"Kirk to *Enterprise*."

"Scott here, Captain."

"Returning to ship. Beam us up, Mr. Scott."

The Council gallery disappeared in dazzle.

Twelve hours.

Kirk moved restlessly in his command chair. The decision that confronted him was no joke. Twelve hours—and all plant life on Marak II would be irreversibly on its way to becoming extinct. Seven hundred and twenty minutes to allow the plague to complete its lethal work—or to persuade Ardana to make good on its pledge of the zenite consignment.

He swung his chair around to Uhura. "Advise Starfleet Command that the methods being employed by the government of Ardana will not make the zenite available. It is my view that I have only one alternative. I hereby notify that I must try to reason directly with the Troglyte miners. I am assuming full responsiblity for these direct negotiations."

McCoy walked over to him and laid a hand on Kirk's shoulder. "That won't be easy, Jim. Ardana has supplied us with data showing mental inferiority in the Troglytes."

"That's impossible, Bones! They have accepted personal sacrifice for a common cause. Mentally inferior beings aren't capable of that much abstract loyalty."

"I've checked the findings thoroughly," McCoy said gently. "Their intellect ratings are almost twenty percent below the planetary average."

Spock turned from his hooded computer. "But they all belong to the same species," he reminded McCoy. "Those who live on Stratos and those who live below all originated on the surface, not long ago. It is basic biological law that their physical and mental evolution must have been similar."

"True enough, Spock. But obviously the ancestors of those who live on Stratos had left the environment of the mines. That's how they avoided further effects of their influence."

"What influence?" Kirk asked.

McCoy held out a small sealed container, carefully.

"This is a low zenite ore sample I had brought from the surface. If I unsealed the container, it would have detrimental effects on everybody here."

"Zenite is shipped all over the galaxy wherever there's danger of plant plague," Spock protested. "No side effects have been reported."

"After it's refined there are none. But in its natural state it emits an odorless, invisible gas which retards the cortical functioning of the brain. At the same time it heightens emotional imbalance, causing violent reactions."

"Then the mines must be full of this gas," Kirk said.

McCoy nodded. "And the Troglytes breath it constantly."

"But the Disruptors—Vanna, for instance. They've outwitted a highly organized culture, apparently for years."

"Captain," Spock said, "you will recall Vanna's experience as a servant in Plasus' household. She was removed from exposure to the gas for an apparently significant period. Perhaps without long exposure, its effects slowly wear off."

"They do," McCoy said. "The other Disruptors probably have similar histories."

"Any way of neutralizing the gas, Bones?"

"No. But filter masks would eliminate the exposure."

"Get one, Bones—or make a mock-up of one, fast—and report back here on the double. Lieutenant Uhura, call Advisor Plasus."

After a considerable interval, the Council gallery materialized on the main viewing screen. Plasus was sitting at the cubical table, drinking slowly.

"Your further communication is not welcome, Captain," he said.

"I may be able to change your mind," Kirk said. "At least, I hope so. My ship's surgeon has made a crucial discovery. He has found that zenite ore discharges a gas that impairs brain function. He thinks he can counteract it."

McCoy appeared at Kirk's elbow, a face mask in

his hand. "That is the case, Mr. Advisor. This filter arrangement in my hand is a gas mask. It eliminates all gases injurious to humanoid life. If others like it are distributed to the miners, we can confidently expect them to achieve intellectual equality with Stratos inhabitants, perhaps quite soon."

Plasus dropped the goblet. "Who are you? Who are you to talk of 'intellectual equality' for—for *Troglytes?*"

"Let me present Dr. McCoy, Medical Officer of the *Enterprise*, Mr. Advisor," Kirk said. "We have checked his findings with our computers. They are absolutely valid."

"Are you saying that this comical mask can accomplish what centuries of evolution have failed to do?"

"Yes. That's what I said, Mr. Advisor."

"Centuries isn't a long time in terms of evolution," McCoy added.

"And do your computers also explain how my ancestors managed to create a magnificence like Stratos City while the Troglytes remained savages?"

"Your ancestors removed themselves from contamination by the gas," Spock said.

"Preposterous!"

"We have no time to argue," Kirk said. "I propose to inform Vanna that the filters are available."

"I doubt that even Vanna will credit such nonsense!"

"Are you afraid that the filters might work, Mr. Advisor?"

Kirk's question obviously hit home. Plasus stamped his foot on the iridescent floor. "You are here to complete an emergency mission, Captain! Not to conduct unauthorized tests!"

"I am here to collect a zenite consignment," Kirk said. "If these masks will help me do it, I will use them."

"I forbid it, Captain! Your Federation orders do not entitle you to defy local governments." Plasus reached for a switch. "This communication is ended."

As he faded from the screen, Kirk said, "My diplomacy seems to be somewhat inadequate."

"Pretty hard to overcome prejudice, Jim."

Kirk nodded. "Doesn't leave us much choice, does it?"

"Not much time, Captain," Spock said. "There are now ten hours and forty minutes left us to deliver the consignment to Marak II."

Kirk took the mask from McCoy. "Alert the Transporter Room to beam me down to Vanna's confinement quarters, Mr. Spock."

"Jim! You're returning to Stratos against government orders?"

"Unless Vanna has something definite to gain for her people, she'll die, Bones, before she turns over the zenite to us."

Spock intervened, an undertone of anxiety in his voice. "If you are apprehended violating the High Advisor's orders, he will consider it within his rights to execute you."

Kirk grinned. "If you're about to suggest that *you* contact Vanna, the answer is negative, Mr. Spock. And that goes for you, too, Bones."

Spock said stiffly, "Allow me to point out that a First Officer is more expendable than either a doctor or a Captain, sir."

"This mission is strictly unofficial," Kirk said. "Nobody is to have any part of it—or take any responsibility for it but myself. That's an order, Mr. Spock."

Silently the Vulcan detached his phaser from his belt and handed it to Kirk. Kirk took it, saying, "You have the con, Mr. Spock. Stand by until I contact you."

Vanna's confinement quarters were narrow, barely wide enough to accommodate a slim sleep dais and a small cube table. Her face still drawn from her ordeal, she was pacing the short length of the cell when she halted in amazement at the sight of him.

"I've brought you a gift," he said, and held out the mask to her. "Listen to me carefully, Vanna. In the mines there's a dangerous gas that affects the development of the Troglytes who are exposed to it too long. This mask will prevent any further damage and allow recovery to take place."

He laid the mask on the table and waited for her surprise to subside. She made no move toward the table.

"Gas from zenite?" she said suspiciously. "It's hard to believe that something we can neither see nor feel can do much harm."

"An idea isn't seen or felt, Vanna. But a mistaken idea is what's kept the Troglytes in the mines all these centuries."

"Will all the Troglytes receive these masks?"

"I will arrange to have Federation engineers help construct them."

She faced him, her eyes pondering. "Suppose Plasus will not agree?"

"Plasus is not the whole government," Kirk said.

"But the City Council will not listen to Troglytes."

"When the zenite is delivered, we'll come back. Then I'll request permission to mediate for the Troglytes. I give you my word."

"Stratos," she said, "was built by leaders who gave their word that all inhabitants would live there. The Troglytes are still waiting."

"This time you won't have to wait," he said gently. "We'll deliver the zenite in a few hours."

Her face was tormented. "Hours can become centuries just as words can be lies."

Kirk grasped her shoulders. "You must trust me, Vanna! If you don't, millions of people will die! A whole planet will die! The zenite is all that can save them—and the masks are all that can save the Troglytes!"

She closed her eyes for a moment, swaying. Then she said, "Very well, Captain. But the consignment is deep in the mines. I cannot tell you how to find it. I must take you to it."

Kirk hesitated. "Valuable hostages" was the phrase Plasus had used. There was no getting away from the fact that Captain James Kirk of the *Enterprise* would qualify as a very valuable hostage. But he had asked for her trust; he would have to give her his. He took out his communicator.

"Kirk to Scott. Beam us both up, and then back down to the mines."

Blinking in the planet's relentlessly glaring sunlight, Kirk drew the mask down over his head. Through its goggles, he could see Vanna's delicate figure, a dark shadow against the darker shadows of the mine's entrance, vanish into blackness. He followed her.

They were moving down a steeply descending tunnel. Ahead of him Kirk could discern faint glimmers of unidentifiable light. Then they were in a large cavern. Its walls glowed greenly with the phosphorescence of zenite ore lodes that etched themselves in cabalistic scribbles on the rock face like messages left by witches. Other jagged rocks jutted from the floor. The cavern might have been an underground graveyard of magicians' tombstones.

A miner's mortae lay against one of the floor's peaked rocks. Picking it up, Vanna struck the rock three times; the rock rang like a gong. As the sound died, Kirk heard a stealthy movement from a narrow ledge high on the left wall of the cave. Two big, begrimed Troglytes were climbing down a series of crude steps, hewed into the rock, to the cavern floor.

Vanna touched their shoulders in greeting. Their faces lightened. "Anka, Midro," she said.

"Vanna. It is you." Anka, the bigger Troglyte, touched her shoulder in similar greeting. "You have returned."

"And I have brought you a hostage," she said. "Seize him!"

The Troglytes grabbed Kirk's arms so swiftly that he could not make a move in defense. They were twisted behind him as Vanna, jerking his phaser from his belt, thrust it into hers. Then she snatched his communicator and hurled it against a sharp-toothed outcropping of rock a few feet away.

Kirk found his voice, but it was unfamiliar, hoarse, distorted by the mask. "We had a bargain. Why are you breaking it?"

"Did you really think I would trust you, Captain?"

"I trusted you," he said.

"You thought you'd tricked me with your talk of unseen gas and filters. I don't believe in it any more than Plasus does."

"Then you are a fool," Kirk said. "The filters can free you just as I said they could."

"Only weapons will free us," she retorted. "And you have just furnished us with two valuable ones. Yourself—and this." She touched the phaser in her belt.

"Holding me will not help you. My men will still come for the zenite consignment."

She laughed. "Without that," she said, pointing to the communicator, "you will be hard to locate."

"They will find me," Kirk said.

"Perhaps." She removed his mask and draped it over a mortae thrust into a crevice on the wall. "I don't think you will be needing this." Then she had a second thought, and taking the mask down again, handed it to Anka. "Send this to Plasus. It will inform him that we have more to bargain with than our mortaes and thongs."

Anka's eyes brightened. "You are clever, Vanna. Very clever."

He hurried out of the cavern and she turned to Midro. "Go to the other mines and tell the Troglytes to post watchers. Search parties may be coming soon."

Midro pointed to Kirk. "What of him?"

Vanna drew the phaser from her belt. "I will see that he does not escape."

"If we kill him," Midro said, "there'll be no need to see to that."

"A dead hostage is useless," she told him.

His face set stubbornly. "Only the Troglytes need know."

"I brought him—and I will say what is to be done."

"You're not the only Disruptor," Midro said sullenly. "I too can say."

"Can you do nothing but argue?" she cried impatiently. "Hurry—or the searchers will be here!"

"When Anka returns, we will *all* say." Nevertheless, he left.

Vanna kept the phaser leveled on Kirk. "Now, Captain, dig," she said. "Dig for zenite as the Troglytes do. I will give you a lesson in what our lives are like."

Silently, Kirk turned to the wall. It proved to be hard work. There was a bag on the floor in which he was told to put the chunks of ore; it took him a long time to get it half full. Vanna watched, smiling, as immaculate Captain James Kirk of the Starship *Enterprise* tore a nail on a bleeding finger.

"Is that what the Disruptors are working for?" he said. "The right to kill everyone?"

"Midro is a child."

"The filter masks could change that."

"Keep digging. You do it well, Captain. The unseen gas doesn't seem to be harming you."

"It takes a while for the effects to become noticeable." He straightened his aching back. "How long do you plan to keep me here? Providing Midro doesn't kill me, of course."

"Until we have help in the mines and our homes in the clouds."

"That might be quite a while." Kirk loosened another chunk of ore. "Longer than I can wait!"

He hurled the rough lump full in her face. She staggered back with a cry, and a moment later Kirk had wrested the phaser from her. He leveled it at the cavern entrance and fired. The boulders supporting it disintegrated, and the whole upper portion of its walls crumbled with a crash, sealing the entrance with a massive pile of rubble.

"You have trapped us!"

"Obviously."

"But soon the atmosphere will go! We will die!"

"Die? From something we cannot see or feel? You

astound me, Vanna." He picked his way over the rubble to his communicator. As he had rather expected, it was unharmed; these instruments had been designed for rough use. "Kirk to *Enterprise.*"

"Spock here, Captain. Is anything wrong?"

"Nothing. Are you locked in on me?"

"Locked in, sir. Ready to beam up consignment."

"Circumstances dictate a slight variation, Mr. Spock." Kirk eyed Vanna warily. "Hold on these coordinates. Locate the High Advisor and beam him down to me immediately. Without advance communication. Repeat—*without advance communication.*"

"Instructions clear, sir. We'll carry through at once. Spock out."

"You will seal Plasus in here also?" Vanna had gone rigid with alarm.

"I am preparing a slight demonstration of the effects of unbelieved gas," Kirk said. He waited. After a moment, the cavern shimmered and Plasus materialized. Such fury shook him when he saw Kirk that at first he failed to register the greenish darkness of his surroundings.

"Abduction of a planetary official is a serious crime, Captain! You will pay for it, I promise!"

Awe struggled with the alarm on Vanna's face. Kirk leveled the phaser at them both. "Not till you're convinced of the effects of zenite gas, Mr. Advisor."

"What effects? I see no change in either of you!"

"You need closer exposure." He waved to the half-filled bag at the cavern wall. "Fill that container."

"You suggest that *I* dig zenite?"

Kirk waved the phaser. "I insist, Mr. Advisor."

Plasus' fists clenched. "You will indeed pay for this, Captain." After eyeing the steady phaser for a moment, he turned to the wall, and began to scrabble at the open zenite lode. It was quickly obvious that he had never done any physical labor before in his life.

Kirk's jaw hardened, and he smiled a cold, thin smile. He felt strangely vindictive, and was enjoying it. "You too, Vanna."

She stared at him for a moment, and then obediently turned also to the wall.

Time passed. After a while, the communicator beeped. "*Enterprise* to Captain."

"What is it, Spock?"

"Contact check, sir. May I remind you that there are only five hours left to—"

"Your orders were to stand by. Carry them out."

"Standing by."

Kirk clicked out. Both his laborers were beginning to show signs of exhaustion. Vanna leaned against the wall for a moment. "I grow faint," she whispered. "The oxygen is going."

"She is right," said Plasus, panting. "You must have us transported out of here."

"Dig."

"You imbecile! We'll die!" Plasus cried.

Kirk backhanded him. "I said, *dig!*"

Knocked back against the wall, arms spread, Plasus snarled, an animal at bay; all trace of the urbane ruler of Ardana had vanished. "I will take no more orders!" He lurched forward.

Kirk jerked the phaser. "Another step and I'll kill you."

Vanna stared at Kirk's distorted face. "Captain—the gas!" she choked out. "You were right! It *is* affecting you!"

Plasus took the cue. "Are you as brave with a mortae as you are with a phaser?" he taunted.

Infuriated, Kirk tossed the phaser to the floor. Plasus scooped two mortae from the rock ledge, and one in each hand, charged Kirk like a clumsy bull, slashing. Kirk dodged, grabbed Plasus' right wrist and tumbled him with a karate twist. The head struck rock. The two mortae clanged on the floor and Kirk leapt for Plasus' throat. As he fell on the High Advisor, the communicator dropped from his belt.

Vanna grabbed it and began shouting. "*Enterprise! Enterprise!*" It remained dead. Vanna shook it, and then found the switch. "*Enterprise!* Help! They will kill each other! Help us."

For a moment, nothing happened. Kirk's fingers tightened on Plasus' throat. Then the cavern shimmered out of existence, and he found himself wrestling on the Transporter platform of the *Enterprise*.

"Captain!" Spock's voice shouted. "Stop! The gas—"

Kirk let go and got groggily to his feet. "The gas? What gas?" He looked around, almost without recognition. The Transporter Room was full of armed security guards. Vanna was cowering; Plasus was crawling off the platform, all defiance fled. It had been a near thing.

The Council gallery of Stratos City resembled a first rehearsal reading of a play, Kirk thought. The whole cast was assembled. He hoped they had all learned their lines.

"I understand you are going to get what you came for," Plasus said.

"Yes, Mr. Advisor."

"The zenite will be delivered exactly as I agreed," Vanna said.

But Plasus hadn't yet learned all his lines. He turned on her. "The word 'agreed' is not in the Troglyte vocabulary."

"The Captain will have his zenite."

"No thanks to any agreement by you. It had to be obtained by force."

"Force has served your purpose at times," she said.

"And bribery," Plasus said, stubborn to the last. "Those masks."

Kirk had had enough. "The masks will be very effective, Mr. Advisor. The Troglytes will no longer suffer mental retardation and emotional imbalance."

"No," said Plasus. "They will all be like this one—ungrateful and vindictive."

As he spoke, two sentinels entered the gallery staggering under the weight of an immense box. "There," Vanna said, "is the zenite. My word is kept."

"As mine will be," Kirk said. "Thank you, Vanna." He took out his communicator. "Kirk to *Enterprise* . . .

Mr. Scott, the zenite is here in the Council gallery. Have it beamed up immediately . . . Mr. Spock—"

He broke off. Spock and Droxine had drifted to the balustrade. The hand of Ardana's incomparable work of art was on Spock's arm.

"I don't like 'filters' or even 'masks,'" she was saying. "I think the word 'protectors' is much better, don't you, Mr. Spock?"

"It is less technical," he told her. "And therefore, less accurate." He looked down at the hand on his arm. "But perhaps it is more generally descriptive of their function."

"'Protectors' is more personal," she said. "I shall be the first to test them. I shall go down into the mines. I no longer wish to be limited to the clouds."

"There is great beauty in what lies below. And there is only one way to experience it, madame."

"Is your planet like this?" She looked up at him.

"Vulcan is quite different," Spock said. His back was stiff.

"Someday, I should like to see it."

"You cannot remain on Stratos," Spock replied, "if you wish to make a real test of . . . a protector."

Kirk judged it time to intervene. "Mr. Spock, I think it is time. We've got just three hours to get the zenite to Marak II."

Spock turned from the balustrade. Removing the white hand from his arm, he bowed over it. Then he straightened.

"To be exact, Captain," he said, "two hours and fifty-nine minutes."

THE MARK OF GIDEON

(George F. Slavin and Stanley Adams)

"It appears to be Paradise, Mr. Spock," said Kirk, handing back the folder of Federation reports and stepping onto the Transporter platform. "It's taken Gideon long enough to agree to negotiating membership in the Federation."

"I'll be interested in hearing your description, Captain," said Spock, taking his place at the console. "Since they have not permitted any surveillance, or any visitors, you appear to be uniquely privileged to visit Heaven early."

"You won't have long to wait," said Kirk. Uhura's voice replied at once to Spock's request for coordinates. Spock set the levers at 875; 020; 079.

"Let's go, Mr. Spock."

"Energizing, Captain." Spock did not, of course, smile at Kirk's eagerness to be off.

The Transporter Room shimmered, then steadied. Nothing seemed to have happened.

"Mr. Spock," said Kirk, stepping from the platform. "Mr. Spock?" There was no one in the Transporter Room but himself.

He clicked the intercom button. "Mr. Spock, I have not been transported down, and why have you left your post before confirming? Mr. Spock, answer me . . ."

This was not at all according to regulations. Annoyed, Kirk stamped out of the Transporter Room and headed purposefully toward the bridge. There was nobody there either.

He hit the intercom with increasing irritation. "This is the Captain speaking. All bridge personnel report immediately." He folded his arms and waited; there had better be one hell of an explanation. Nothing happened. He switched on the intercom again, alternately calling Engineering, security, Dr. McCoy, and listening. There was only silence.

"Lieutenant Uhura, report to the bridge immediately."

The viewing screen showed only the planet Gideon exactly as he had just seen it before stepping onto the Transporter, a perfectly ordinary M-type planet peacefully poised in the screen. The readouts and lights on the bridge consoles continued to operate in their usual conformations.

"Captain Kirk." The smooth voice of Prime Minister Hodin emerged from the communication screen. "The Council is still awaiting your arrival."

A plump figure rose to its feet from among the Councillors of Gideon.

"This discourtesy is unforgivable!" he snapped. "Doesn't your Federation recognize that first impressions are most important?"

Spock blinked. "Captain Kirk was transported down minutes ago, sir."

"That's impossible."

"I transported him myself," said Spock firmly.

"He never arrived here," said Hodin, evenly. Spock stared at Scott, and turned back to the screen.

"He was beamed directly to your Council Chamber. Please check your coordinates, Prime Minister."

Hodin read out from a slip of paper, "875; 020; 079."

Scott nodded.

"Somethings' gone wrong with the Transporter," said Chekov. "Captain Kirk's lost somewhere between the *Enterprise* and Gideon." His voice rose; Spock's expression remained impassive. The planet hung in the viewscreen, enigmatic.

The Prime Minister was speaking insistently. "We provided you with the exact coordinates for this room, Mr. Spock. And that is all we were obligated to do. If he is not here it is your own responsibility and that of your staff."

"I do not deny that, Your Excellency. I was not attempting to blame your personnel."

"We are glad to hear that, sir." Hodin's voice sounded almost smug. "We are, in fact, inserting it into the records of this . . . most unfortunate event."

"Your Excellency, with intricate machinery so delicately balanced as ours, there is always a margin for error," Spock said sharply. "Captain Kirk may have materialized in some other part of Gideon."

Hodin said, "Let's hope it was dry land, Mr. Spock."

"Your Excellency, to cut directly to the point, I request permission to beam down and search for the Captain."

Hodin sat back, hands on the table before him. "Permission denied, Mr. Spock. Your Federation is well aware of our tradition of isolation from all contaminating contact with the violence of other planets . . ."

"Your Excellency, the wars between star systems no longer prevail in our galaxy. If you will grant permission . . ."

"We shall institute a search immediately. In the meantime I suggest you look to your machinery."

"We have already done so, sir." Spock's voice was now extremely controlled. "With regard to permission to land . . ."

But the Council Chamber had vanished from the screen.

"We must once and for all acknowledge that the purpose of diplomacy is to prolong a crisis," said Spock, deliberately closing the switch.

"What are we waiting for, Mr. Spock? *We're* not diplomats," McCoy flung himself on a chair.

"We are representatives of the Federation, Doctor."

"That doesn't mean we have to sit here like schoolchildren and listen to a damfool lecture by some ... dip-lo-mat."

"Unfortunately, diplomacy is the only channel open to us at the moment. This planet is shielded from our sensors; we cannot observe it. Therefore we are unable to select coordinates. They have to be given to us. We are bound by Federation's agreements with Gideon." Spock turned to Lt. Uhura. "Contact Starfleet immediately. Advise them of this problem and request permission to use every means at our disposal to locate the Captain."

"D'ye think he's there, Spock?" said Scott. "Or are there any other possibilities?"

"They are endless, Mr. Scott."

"Where do we start?" said McCoy helplessly.

Spock leaned over Sulu's console. "Institute three-hundred-and-sixty degree scan, Mr. Sulu—one degree at a time."

"You're going to scan space for him? But sir, that could take years!"

"Then the sooner you begin, Mr. Sulu, the better," said Spock grimly.

Sweating slightly, Kirk ran from the elevator and pressed a door; it did not budge. He tried to force it with no success. He tried the next door; it opened easily. Standing guardedly in the opening, he pushed it all the way open with his elbow, one hand on the butt of his phaser. It whished slightly in the silence. The tables in the lounge stood as though the crew had just been summoned; a half-finished chess game, a sandwich with a bite out of it, a book dropped carelessly on the floor. But the only sound was Kirk's own breathing. He went out into the corridor again, warily.

Two more doors, locked. The third, labeled "Captain's Quarters," opened to the lightest pressure. His familiar room suddenly seemed alien—no crackle from the intercom, the bunk neatly made up, his books orderly on their shelf; his lounging robe swung eerily in the slight breeze made by the opening door. Momentarily disoriented, he wondered for a wild moment whether he had strayed from his own body and was visiting the *Enterprise* long after he and his crew had perished from the universe.

Footsteps! Dancing footsteps, echoing in the corridor; he pivoted on his now very real heels and stared. At the end of the hall a graceful figure whirled and curtsied, feet pattering gaily on the utilitarian flooring.

She caught sight of Kirk in mid-pirouette, and stopped with a little cry. He reached, and caught her; the sight of a human form brought his sense of reality back with a bump.

"Who the . . . who are you?"

She frowned, her delicate forehead lovely even when wrinkling; suddenly she smiled.

"Odona . . . yes. My name is Odona. Why did you bring me here?" She indicated the ship's corridor with a wide gesture.

Kirk was startled. "What are you doing on my ship?"

"This entire ship is yours?"

"It's not my personal property. I'm the Captain."

"And you have all this to yourself?" Her voice was full of wonder.

"At the moment, we seem to have it all to ourselves," Kirk corrected.

Odona smiled, sapphire eyes looking up from under sable lashes. "So it seems. You're hurting me, Captain."

Kirk hastily released her.

"Captain James Kirk. And I did not bring you here, incidentally."

"If you didn't . . ."

"Exactly. Who did?"

She shrugged helplessly. The decorations bordering her brief tunic twinkled in the lights.

"What happened before you got here?" said Kirk. "Try to remember. It's important."

She puzzled over it for a moment. "I remember . . . it seems I was standing in a very large auditorium, crowded with people, thousands of people pressed against me so hard I could hardly breathe . . . I was fighting for breath, screaming to get out and they kept pushing and pushing . . ." She shuddered.

"Don't be afraid." Kirk placed a comforting hand on her shoulder.

"I'm not." She looked up at him. "But you are troubled?"

Kirk turned away. "I am the only one of my crew left on the *Enterprise*. Out of four hundred and thirty. I may be the only one left alive."

"I am sorry. If only I could help."

"You can," said Kirk earnestly. "Tell me the rest. You were fighting for breath, screaming to get out, and . . ."

"And suddenly I was here on this . . . your ship. And there is so much room, so much freedom. I just wanted to float." She smiled impishly. "And then, there you were."

"How long have you been on the *Enterprise*?" Kirk's questions were almost random; any clue, any train of suggestion, might lead him to a solution.

"I don't know. Not long. Does it matter?"

"It might. Come on." He started back toward the bridge.

Odona followed reluctantly.

"Do we have to leave this wonderful open place?"

Kirk glowered at the chronometer in the bridge, gripping Odona's hand. She tried to pull away from him; he held her firmly.

"Half an hour of my life is lost."

Odona stared at him.

"Between the time I tried to leave this ship for Gideon, and the time I found myself here alone, a full half hour disappeared—poof! What happened during that half hour?"

"What is Gideon?"

"Your home, the planet you came from . . . don't you remember?"

"I don't know any Gideon." She looked at him, apparently utterly lost.

"That's impossible. We were in synchronous orbit over the capital city. I was supposed to beam down. Something went wrong. You must have been sent aboard from Gideon."

She shook her head, trying to remember.

"I do not think so."

Kirk flipped on the viewing screen. Gideon had vanished. The changing patterns of the stars indicated the forward motion of the ship. Odona moved closer, and put her hand in his.

"We are no longer over Gideon," said Kirk in a flat voice.

"Where are we?"

"I don't know. I don't recognize that quadrant," said Kirk dully.

Odona bit her lip. Thinking aloud, Kirk said, "Odona, you must realize that we are not here together by accident. Someone must have arranged it, for a purpose, an unknown purpose."

A small voice replied, "Captain Kirk, before I said I wasn't afraid. Now, I think I am."

He looked at her with compassion, and they turned back to the incomprehensible pattern of stars.

"Go back two degrees, there was a pulse variation," said Spock. Sulu maneuvered the sensor screen.

"There," said Spock. "There is something. Give me a reading."

Sulu flicked switches. "I can't make it out, sir."

"Get chemical analysis and molecular structure."

Sulu pointed silently at the indicators. Scott, McCoy and Chekov watched anxiously. Spock shook his head.

"Space debris."

Sulu sighed, and resumed tracking.

"Lieutenant Uhura, has Starfleet honored our request with an answer?"

"Not yet, sir."

"Did you impress upon them that the Captain's life is at stake?"

"Of course, Mr. Spock," she said indignantly. "But they insisted that the matter had to be referred to the Federation."

"What department?"

"Bureau of Planetary Treaties, sir."

"Contact them directly."

"I already have, Mr. Spock. They insist we go though Starfleet channels."

Sulu exploded, spinning in his chair. "With the Captain missing that's the best they could come up with?"

"A bureaucrat," said Spock bitterly, "is the opposite of a diplomat. But they manage to achieve the same results."

He stared at the chronometer. The second indicator clicked on. The captain was waiting . . . somewhere. And time was passing inalterably.

Suddenly Uhura's voice broke the tense silence.

"Mr. Spock, Gideon is making contact."

McCoy said sourly, "Now we're in for another dose of doubletalk."

"Since we must learn the language of diplomacy in order to deal with our present problem, shall we just listen to what they have to tell us?" said Spock. "Then, Doctor, we can decide on the relative merits of their statements."

Four poker-faced ministers flanked the Prime Minister as he appeared on the viewer. Courteously, Spock began, "Your Excellency, we are pleased to hear that you have news of the Captain."

"Good news!" said the smiling image. "Very good news indeed, Mr. Spock. Your Captain is definitely *not* on Gideon. We have made a thorough search, just as you requested. I am sure you will be relieved to know you may now proceed to investigate all the other possibilities, and forget about Gideon."

"But that is not what we requested!"

"It is in the records, Mr. Spock," broke in the voice

of the Prime Minister. "You asked for a thorough search of Gideon. We have used every means at our disposal to accommodate you, Mr. Spock." Outraged astonishment overlaid the diplomat's usual smile.

"Your record on this subject cannot be precise, Excellency."

Hodin waved to an assistant, and took from him a thick book. With ambitious eagerness the assistant had already opened it to a specific passage.

"You do not intend, I hope, that a conference be made the subject of a dispute between Gideon and the Federation, Mr. Spock."

"Your Excellency, a dispute is farthest from our minds. It's quite unnecessary to check your documents. I am merely suggesting to you that the language of our request may not have been understood exactly as intended."

Hodin stood up, huffily indignant. He waved his puffy hand.

"Mr. Spock, you are an officer of a spaceship. In your profession you make use of many instruments, tools, and . . . weapons . . . to achieve your objectives, do you not?"

"Yes, sir."

Hodin's eyes were squinting with an apparent effort to remain diplomatically cool. His posture betrayed him.

"However," he continued, "the only tool diplomacy has is language. It is of the utmost importance that the meaning be crystal clear."

Spock's own posture was of stiff attention.

"I am basically a scientist, Excellency. Clarity of formulation is essential in my profession also."

"I am glad to hear that. Perhaps then you will make a greater effort to choose your words precisely."

The word "precisely" vibrated through the bridge like a red petticoat in a bullring. The crew was coming to a full boil; all hands were fists by now.

McCoy muttered, "Are you going to let him get away with that, Spock?"

"No matter what you say, he'll find a way to twist the meaning," said Scott.

Uhura growled, "How can you stand this, Mr. Spock?"

McCoy leaned past Spock to the viewer and spoke directly to Hodin. "Our Captain is lost out there somewhere. We don't care how much you have searched, we are going over every inch of space ourselves. He's got to be down there somewhere. We're going after him!"

Too loudly, Chekov said, "This is no time to stick to rules and regulations, this is an emergency!" McCoy gently pulled him back, and leaned toward the screen again.

"We can't leave without being absolutely positive ourselves that everything has been done," he said. "Surely you can understand our feelings."

Hodin turned back to the screen, smiling.

"Mr. Spock. Mr. Spock."

"Yes, Your Excellency?"

"Are you still there?" That smile was imperturbable. "There was considerable interference with your transmission. A great deal of noise drowned out your transmission; could you please repeat more clearly?"

McCoy retreated, baffled. "Let me apologize for the *noise*, Your Excellency," said Spock. "To summarize, I request permission to transport down to Gideon."

The Prime Minister looked at his deputies and back at Spock. They all burst out in offensive laughter.

"Forgive me, Mr. Spock," Hodin's oily voice resumed. "No criticism of your equipment is intended. But evidently it has sent your Captain on some strange journey—we all still hope a safe one, of course." He bowed formally. "But it could create for us a grave incident with your Federation. And now you propose to repeat the disaster with yet another officer? Are you mad?"

Scott shouted, "I'll not take that, Mr. Spock. The Transporter was in perfect condition . . . I pairsonally guarantee that mysel'. Transport me down there this minute and I'll be proving it to those . . . those . . . gentlemen!"

The chill in Spock's quick glance froze Scott in his tracks.

"I could not quite make that out, Mr. Spock. Would you be so good as to repeat what you said?" Hodin gave every appearance of amusement at the antics of the crew.

"The ship's engineer was saying that the malfunction that existed has now been repaired," said Spock, a quelling eye on Scott. "We would like to test it immediately. I would like to transport down to your Council Chamber."

"But, Mr. Spock, you . . ."

Spock interrupted Hodin. "Your Excellency, grant this one request."

"You are a very persistent fellow, Mr. Spock."

A moment of tension passed while Hodin again consulted with his staff.

"All right, Mr. Spock." A whistling sound passed through the bridge as the entire crew released held breath. "You shall test the skill of your . . . er . . . very excitable repairman."

Scott's teeth ground in Chekov's ear. "He doesna ken what excitable is . . ." Chekov grinned at him, and whispered, "But he's letting him go . . . Wait."

"There is one further proviso. We cannot risk additional incident. You will therefore transport a member of my staff to your ship. Let us first see if that works."

"Thank you, Your Excellency. Your proposal is accepted." Spock turned to Scott. "Transporter Room, Mr. Scott, on the double."

"At once, Mr. Spock," said Scott, rather stiffly. He stalked to the elevator and punched the door.

On the screen, yet another assistant with a large book was talking to Hodin, who looked up.

"My assistant will provide you with the proper, what is the word?"

"Co-or-di-nates," said Spock, very clearly.

"Thank you. You may proceed."

The Gideonite assistant placed himself at a corner of the Council Chamber.

"875," he said.

"875, Mr. Scott," said Spock.

"875, aye."

"020."

"020."

"709."

"709?" The last number was repeated. Spock hesitated for a moment.

"709, Mr. Scott. Energize."

"Mr. Spock, the young gentleman fron Gideon is here," Scott reported triumphantly.

"Very good, Mr. Scott." Spock turned to the screen. "Your assistant is safely arrived, Your Excellency. And now we would like to send down myself and if possible, a few technicians to follow through on . . ."

"Now, now, now, Mr. Spock. Not so fast. That is quite a different matter. We agreed to allow one representative on our soil, your Captain alone. Now you suggest a 'few technicians.' And will the Federation then demand an army of 'technicians' to hunt for these?"

Patiently, Spock said, "I will demand only one thing, Prime Minister; that I be permitted to beam down to your planet to search for the Captain."

"Your request," said Hodin, smoothly triumphant, "will be brought to the floor at the next session of Gideon's Council. Er . . . do not look forward to a favorable reply."

"Your Excellency!" Spock pressed the switch several times rapidly; the screen remained blank. He hit the intercom.

"Mr. Scott. Send the gentleman from Gideon home."

"I was just beginning to think you might find a new career as a diplomat, Spock," said McCoy.

"Do not lose hope, Doctor. Lt. Uhura, contact Starfleet Command. Demand an instant reply to our request for permission to land on Gideon."

The room was tense as Uhura operated her console.

"*Enterprise* to Starfleet Command.

"*Enterprise* to Starfleet Command."

"*Enterprise* to Starfleet Command." Kirk and Odona bent over the console, Kirk's fingers expertly flicking the controls.

"Captain Kirk here. Red Priority Alert. Do you read me? Red Priority Alert." The console impassively continued its normal light patterns.

"Isn't it working?" said Odona.

"It seems to be all right." Kirk flipped the manual control and held it open.

"Kirk here. Answer please. Red Priority Alert."

"If it is working someone must hear you," Odona said hopefully.

"There's nothing. If they do hear they aren't replying."

"Why would they do that?"

"They wouldn't." Kirk glanced quizzically at her, then crossed the bridge to Sulu's board. With a few swift motions he altered the setting so that the lights showed a different pattern.

"I'm taking the ship out of warp speed."

"Out of what?" Odona looked utterly baffled.

Kirk laughed. "Space terminology. We're no longer moving faster than light. I trimmed her down to sublight speed till we can find out where we are."

"It doesn't feel any different."

"Well, no." Kirk was amused. Abruptly, his smile faded. "Maybe it isn't." He stared at the other consoles, one by one. No change was apparent. He turned on the forward viewing screen. No motion was visible in the star-filled sky, still and remote.

"Has the ship slowed down?"

"If we can believe the screen, it has."

"Oh, don't tell me the *sky* is out of order now!"

They stood side by side watching the glittering heavens; behind them the console lights moved in rhythmic silence. Odona said softly, "It's so quiet, and peaceful."

"It isn't really, you know. Out there, it's . . ." As he turned his head to look at her he felt fingers against his lips.

"And it's beautiful," she said.

Kirk looked back at the panoply on the screen, and at the delicate oval face in its black wings of hair.

"And it's beautiful. Very beautiful."

"We're all alone here. Can it last a long, long time?" Her eyes were raised to his, sparkling. His arm slipped around her.

"How long would you like it to last?"

"Forever." Odona's voice was barely audible.

"Let's see now. Power; that's no problem, it regenerates. Food; we had a five years' supply for four hundred and thirty. For two of us that should last . . ."

"Forever?"

Their eyes met, and her hands touched his shoulders. He pulled her closer. She said in a trembling voice, "All my life I've dreamed of being alone . . ."

The startling intensity of her "alone" woke Kirk; the moment was broken. Gently he released her. She stood, her arms still raised, eyelids lowered, her expression rapt.

"Most people are afraid of being alone," Kirk said.

She opened her eyes and looked him in the face.

"Where I live people dream of it."

"But why? What makes the people of Gideon dream of being alone?" His voice had recovered its tone of impersonal interest.

"I . . ." she caught herself. Her expression of puzzlement returned. "Gideon? I told you I don't know where my home is." She shook her head.

"It might well be Gideon." Kirk appraised her coolly.

"Does it matter so much?" She started toward him, her hands out.

"It might help me locate our position." She stopped. Her hands dropped to her sides. She shrugged, almost imperceptibly.

"And then you might find your crew. Being here with you, I forgot there were others. I envy your sense of loyalty." She drew close to him. "I wish I could ease your fear for your friends."

Kirk shook his head. "I *must* make contact with whoever is manipulating us. I've got to find a way . . ." He paced the room, stopping in front of each of the consoles, willing them to reveal something, the smallest clue. Suddenly he whirled and faced the girl.

"Odona, can't you remember why your people want so much to be alone?"

A wave of utter panic swept over her face. She shivered, although there was no change in the temperature.

"Because they cannot ever be."

"Why not?"

"There are so many." He could hardly hear her reply. She lifted her head. A shuddering force seemed to rise from her slender body.

"So many . . . so many. There is no place, no street, no house, no garden, no beach, no mountain that is not filled with people. If he could, each one would kill to find a place to be alone. If he could, he would die for it."

She stared at him, tears creeping down her cheeks, supporting herself on Uhura's chair. She looked exhausted.

"Why were you sent here, Odona?" Kirk put the question compassionately.

Her head lifted proudly. "No one commands Odona. I was not sent here."

Kirk strode to her side, and took her face in his hands.

"Have you come here to kill?"

Her tearstained face was shocked; unable to answer, her lips formed a soundless "no."

"Have you come here to die?"

"I don't know. I don't care . . . I only know I am here. I only know I am happy here." She threw her arms around his neck and clung to him, desperately. The trouble in her eyes moved Kirk as her coquetry had failed to do. He kissed her, gently, then more urgently. Yet in the back of his mind the images evoked by her tormented outcry haunted him; faces of people yearning for solitude, young, old, men, women and children unable to draw a breath that was not their neighbor's.

The stars on the viewscreen ignored them.

Suddenly Kirk drew back his arm with an exclamation. She flinched.

"I have done something wrong?"

"No." Kirk smiled ruefully. But he let her go, and pulled up his sleeve. There was a bruise on his forearm. Blood made a tiny dome in its center.

"Why does it take so long?" Odona asked, peering at it.

"Long? What?"

"The bruise. It stays the same."

"And the irritation gets worse. If Dr. McCoy were here he'd take care of it with a simple wave of his medical tricorder."

It was obviously the same as if he had said "his wand" to Odona, but she said, "I would willingly give up some of this glorious space to Dr. McCoy, if he could take away your . . . irritation."

"They took Dr. McCoy, but they had to leave Sickbay," said Kirk. He took her arm and steered her to the elevator.

On the bridge of the other *Enterprise*, Uhura, Chekov, Scott and McCoy were intently scanning the viewscreen. Spock stood at attention in the Captain's position. Over the air the voice of the Starfleet Admiral, slightly distorted by its long journey, sounded extremely stern.

"I sympathize deeply, but Starfleet cannot override Federation directives in this matter."

"The crew will not understand it, Admiral."

"Damn straight," muttered McCoy.

"Has your crew suddenly become interested in provoking a war, Mr. Spock? That is hardly Starfleet's mission."

"We only want to save the life of the Captain," repeated Spock.

"You have not proved your case to the Federation, or even to Starfleet, for that matter," said the Admiral.

"What's the matter wi' them all?" said Scott in a surly voice. "Ye'd think naebody but us care at all . . ."

Spock shushed him with a wave of his hand behind his back.

"I'm positive I will be able to do so to your satisfaction, Admiral. It has been clear to me since my first exchange of, er . . . courtesies with the Prime Minister that they have taken the Captain prisoner."

"Granted, Mr. Spock."

"I know now precisely where the Captain is being held." A stunned silence gripped the crew.

"Leave it to Spock, every time," whispered Uhura. Scott nodded.

". . . If he is at the same place to which we transported him," Spock went on.

"They would not dare to harm him in the Council Chamber!" The Admiral was outraged.

"That is not where the Captain is, Admiral. He is being held nearby."

"Well! You have now answered What and Where. I now await your explanation of Why."

"Since this planet is shielded from our sensors, by Federation agreement, Admiral, we cannot possibly establish that without on-the-spot investigation."

"Mhm. What evidence have you that the Captain's life is threatened?"

"Why else would they keep him?"

"I'm afraid that's not good enough, Mr. Spock. Permission denied."

Spock took a deep breath, fists clenched. "I wish personally to go on record that this decision is completely arbitrary."

"So noted." The screen blipped off.

"Diplomats!" exploded Scott. "What did you mean,

Mr. Spock? Didn't we beam the Captain into the Council Chamber?"

"Quiet, please!" Mr. Spock broke through the agitated babble. "No, Mr. Scott, Gideon supplied us with two different sets of coordinates; one for the Captain, and one for our . . . er . . . recent guest." As Scott looked doubtful, he said, "The Captain's Log is evidence enough—I hope." He turned to the ship's memory. The crew stared at the numbers on the readout.

"You're right, Mr. Spock!"

"Look at that!"

"What kind of finagle is this?" Scott turned to Spock, hands on hips and a glare in his eye.

"What now, Mr. Spock?" said McCoy. "Are we to sit here and wait with our hands folded for the Captain to reappear?"

"This is typical of top echelon isolation." Spock's dry voice conveyed disgust. "They are too far away from the elements that influence crew morale."

"At times like this I don't think they remember that there is such a thing," said McCoy furiously.

"It is unfortunate. But for the first time in my career, I am forced to violate a direct order from Starfleet."

"Hear, hear!" shouted Scott. "That's absolutely the right decision, Spock. I'm with you!"

"One hundred percent!" That was Chekov; it was very clear that if Starfleet Command could but hear them the entire crew would be tried for insubordination—at the least.

"I shall beam down there at once." Spock's resolute calm stirred everybody into action; positions were taken.

"Mr. Scott, the con is yours."

"Aye, but ye'll be needing me along," said Scott, protesting.

"The Captain will be needing all of you at your posts." This reminder had the desired effect; subdued, Scott headed for the elevator behind Spock.

"It might be taken as an invasion," McCoy whispered to Scott. "I'll pick up my medical tricorder and meet you in the Transporter Room, Mr. Spock."

"No, Dr. McCoy; I cannot assume responsibility for ordering a fellow officer to violate a Starfleet directive. I go alone."

"Well, that's just about the worst decision you'll ever make, Spock," grumbled McCoy. "I hope you won't regret it."

As he entered the elevator, Spock said, "I'm sure this won't take long." McCoy held out his hand in a good-luck gesture. Spock shook it solemnly, and the doors closed.

"Isn't that just what Captain Kirk said?"

Chekov's words echoed in the suddenly quiet room.

Odona wandered around Sickbay, fingering pieces of equipment, peering curiously at instruments, spelling out the names of chemicals.

"If I can find a medical tricorder I'll be cured in no time," said Kirk, rummaging in a cabinet.

"Cured?"

"My arm," said Kirk patiently. "The pain would be gone."

"Oh. What will happen if you do not find it? Will you become sick? Will you, uh, die?"

Kirk looked at her, astonished. "Of this little scratch? Of course not. It would heal itself, eventually. It's just a simple . . ." He looked closely at the little wound.

"Or is it?" Recollections of biological sampling, blood tests, other scientifically motivated wounds went through his mind. Had someone wanted something of his tissues? Well, there was no telling. He turned back to the cabinet.

"All this is needed to cure those who are . . . sick?" Odona was examining the autoclave. Kirk nodded.

"It is cruel. Why are they not allowed to die?"

"What did you say?"

"Why don't you let them die?"

Her hand lay on the cauterizer; Kirk jumped.

"Don't touch that!"

He was a fraction of a second too late; Odona had

bumped the switch; a jet of flame streaked out. Kirk jerked her away from the machine and switched off the flame in one motion.

"Are you hurt?"

"Just my hand." Odona had not even blinked, had not cried out. Was this a spartan self-control—or something else?"

"Let me see it." She covered her damaged hand.

"It's nothing."

He pulled the hand gently but firmly into the light. Her forefinger was burnt completely away.

"My God!" Kirk's grip tighted with sympathetic horror. She withdrew her hand.

"The pain is already gone. Don't worry." Her voice was quite calm.

"Sutures . . . it's already cauterized . . . shock . . ." Kirk plunged at the cabinet.

"Wait." She was utterly unperturbed. "It's already healing."

Kirk glanced at the hand she held out to him and lurched into the cabinet door. A tiny forefinger had already appeared where a moment ago had been a raw wound. As he goggled, the finger grew before his eyes. In a matter of minutes Odona's hand was as whole as ever.

"See?" she said. "Why did you worry so much? This is strange to you?"

"Regeneration . . ." he muttered. "Injuries heal themselves?"

"Just as your arm will," she said, reassuringly.

"No. I have never seen anything like this before. Do all your people have this capacity?"

"Of course."

"They do not fall sick. Or die."

Once again the fleeting expression of panic swept over her face.

"That is why they long for death," Kirk said slowly, gazing at her. "So many, no one ever dying . . ."

He became aware of a sound—a sound not due to his own or Odona's movements. It grew in his consciousness to a steady throb.

"Do you hear that?" he asked. Odona nodded. Kirk prowled the room, listening at the walls for the direction of the sound. He checked his watch; it timed at seventy-two beats per minute. Odona put her hand to her forehead.

"It sounds like an engine," she offered.

"The ship's engine makes no sound."

"But there is something wrong with the equipment. Could that be it?"

"I know every sound on this ship; this is coming from outside," said Kirk, trying to recollect what the timing had reminded him about.

"Is it a storm?"

"We wouldn't hear a storm in here. Come along, it's not coming from here, at any rate."

They moved cautiously along the corridor, Kirk leading the girl by the hand. Her hand was cold, and a little damp. She must be terrified. The pulse of sound went on, no louder and no less. Kirk stopped at a viewing port in the observation corridor.

"We can see outside from here—if it works." He depressed a button. Nothing happened. He reached for the manual control lever. The panel slid open.

To his horrified amazement, the port was filled with the faces he had imagined when Odona had burst out with her passionate yearning for solitude. Silently screaming, the faces filled his vision with distress and longing. He fell back a step, glanced at Odona. When he looked at the screen again it showed only the still and starlit skies.

Sharply he asked, "What did you see?"

"People . . . the faces of people; and stars."

She turned to him, pale. "What is it? What's happening?"

The sound stopped as suddenly as it had begun. He remembered; the beat had been identical with the human heartbeat. Thousands of people outside the ship, pressing against it with their bodies.

"You said we were moving through space."

"Yes."

"Then there couldn't really be people out there."

"There could," Kirk said grimly. "Someone could be creating an illusion in our minds. Why would they want to do that, Odona?"

She shrank from him. He saw that her forehead was beaded with perspiration.

"I don't know. I don't know anything. Why do you ask me?"

"I wonder . . . if we were convinced of a location, we would stop searching. We might be content to stay here, mightn't we?"

"Be . . . content." Odona's pallor belied her calm. Suddenly he was irritated and tired of trickery.

"Where is my crew, girl? Are they dead? Have you killed them to have the ship to yourself?"

She shivered in his grasp, scarlet patches flaming her cheeks. Her sapphire eyes had lost their sparkle, looked dull and sunken.

"No, no, I don't know anything. Please, Captain, something strange is happening to me. I never felt like this . . ."

"Neither have I," said Kirk, as cold as ice.

"Am I sick? Is this . . . dying?" she whispered, clinging to a doorframe. Her weight fell on Kirk's arms as he gripped her firmly.

"You do not know of sickness," he said. "You have none on your planet. What kind of . . ."

"Now there will be . . . sickness, now there will be death!" Her voice died in a whisper as she fainted, smiling.

"What the blue . . ." Kirk caught her. Bearing her in his arms he started straight back to Sickbay. As he approached the door he was arrested by the sound of pounding feet coming down the corridor.

"Hodin!"

Guards surrounded him as Hodin ponderously walked toward Kirk and his burden.

"Yes, Captain. Our experiment has passed the first stage."

The explanation would have to wait.

"Let me by," he said urgently. "I must help her."

"No," said Hodin, quietly. "We do not want any of your medicines."

"But she's very ill. Look at her—she needs help, and at once."

"We are grateful for her illness. Thank you, Captain. You have done more than you know for us."

Kirk thought they must be mad. He looked at Odona. Her eyelids fluttered. Hodin spoke gravely.

"My dear daughter, you have done well." He took the limp form from Kirk and turned away. The deputation closed in around the baffled Captin.

"Guard him well, we shall need him for a long time," called Hodin over his shoulder.

In total perplexity Kirk marched along with his guard. What had happened to his crew? This corridor along which they were now walking was unfamiliar; not aboard the *Enterprise*, then. Well, where *was* the *Enterprise*? Why did this diplomat want his daughter to die? Perhaps he could take comfort from the fact that he alone had been tricked; perhaps crew and ship were safe elsewhere. They drew near to the "Captain's Quarters" and he heard voices. He halted, despite the guards' effort to press him along.

"I must see him," came the faint tone of Odona.

"Yes, yes. But now you must lie still." Hodin's voice had lost some of its smoothness. "Do you feel great pain?"

"My arms . . . and . . . thighs . . ."

Avid, yet tender, Hodin said, "What is it like?"

"It is like . . . like when we have seen that the people have no hope, Father. You felt . . . great despair. Your heart was heavy because you could do nothing. It is like that."

"You have great courage, my daughter. I am very proud of you." Hodin closed the door softly behind him. Kirk stepped toward him anxiously.

"Let me see her."

"Not yet."

"You don't know what illness she has. Maybe I can tell."

Hodin looked at him gravely. "We know. She has Vegan choriomeningitis."

"Oh, my God." Kirk stepped back; "If she is not treated at once, within twenty-four hours, she will die. I know; it nearly killed me."

Hodin nodded. "Yes, Captain. We learned of your medical history, as we did the plan of a starship, during the negotiations. We brought you here to obtain the microorganisms."

"So that's how my arm was hurt."

"My apologies. As you have learned, we have no medical practitioners. We were unforgivably awkward to have inflicted pain on you . . ."

"You mean you deliberately infected your own daughter . . ." Overcome with fury, Kirk turned on his guards. His right fist shot out and caught one in the midriff; as he doubled up with a grunt, Kirk lashed out at the other and leaped for the door of Odona's sickroom. But the first man had recovered and dived at Kirk's feet, bringing him down; the second guard pulled him roughly up and dragged him back to Hodin.

"We do not wish to hurt you. You will see her as soon as we are certain she is susceptible."

"You *are* mad!" cried Kirk in frustrated rage.

"No, Captain. We are desperate. Bring him along to the Council Chamber."

The chamber was a scene of excited chatter, the deputies of Gideon's government descending upon Hodin, demanding, "How is she? What has happened?"

Hodin waved them to their places around the table. Kirk was brought forward between his guards.

"Your report to the Federation was a tissue of lies," he said angrily. "You described Gideon as a Paradise."

"And so it was . . . once. A long time ago it was as we described it. In the germ-free atmosphere of Gideon people flourished in physical and spiritual perfection, Captain. The life-span was extended and extended, until finally death comes only to the very ancient, when regeneration is no longer possible.

These gifts, Captain, have been our reward for respecting life."

"Most people would envy you."

"We no longer find this condition enviable. Births have increased our population until Gideon is encased in a living mass of beings without rest, without peace, without joy."

"Then why have you not introduced measures to make your people sterile?"

"They do not work," said Hodin simply. "All known techniques are defeated by our organs' capacity to regenerate, like my daughter's hand."

"There are other ways to prevent conception, however."

"This is our dilemma, Captain. Life is sacred to our people. This is the one unshakable tradition. Yet we pay for the gifts that the worship of life has brought us, and the price is very heavy. Because of our overwhelming love of life we have the gifts of regeneration and longevity."

"And misery."

"That is the contradiction."

"The reality, Hodin."

Hodin flinched. He turned his back for a moment, then walked back and forth, the tortured confusion of his mind all too apparent.

"What are we to do? We cannot deny the truth of what has shaped us as we are. We are not capable of interfering with the Creation we love so deeply. It is against our natures."

"Yet you can kill your own daughter. How can you justify that?"

"We are not killing her. It is the disease that will or will not kill her; this is not under our control. The opportunity came to us, perhaps as a gift; we have seized upon it to readjust the life cycle of this planet. My daughter had hoped you might be brought to feel the agony of Gideon, Captain. It is impossible; no stranger could realize the horror of existence.

"I will not ask you to understand my personal grief;

nor will I parade it to gain your cooperation." Hodin had stopped pacing, and faced Kirk proudly.

"My daughter has won my pride, as she has always had my love. She has freely chosen to take this chance with her life, as all the people of Gideon are free to choose. And she cannot be sure she is right."

"This virus is rare. Where do you intend to get it?" said Kirk, grappling with the first of these problems that he felt able to handle.

The smooth diplomatic mask slipped over Hodin's face. Kirk was suddenly wary.

"Your blood will provide it, Captain. You will be staying here."

Kirk slammed the table with the flat of his hand.

"Not me, Hodin. You have other ways to solve your problem. I do not offer my life for this purpose at all; I have other commitments. And I have other hopes for Odona than death."

"My daughter hoped you would love her—enough to stay."

Kirk looked hard at him. "What passed between your daughter and me was between us alone."

"She pleaded with you to stay."

"You watched us, didn't you?"

Hodin bowed his head in admission. "We are desperate. And privacy is perhaps of less concern to us than to you."

"I'm desperate too, you . . ."

Kirk was interrupted by a buzzer. A message was delivered to Hodin, who raised his head in proud sorrow.

"You may go to her now. She is calling for you. You cannot leave quite yet, Captain, can you?"

"Spock to *Enterprise*. Spock to *Enterprise*."

"Scott here, Mr. Spock."

"Mr. Scott, I am speaking to you from the bridge of the *Enterprise*."

"Ye're what, man?"

"Speaking from the bridge of the *Enterprise*, Mr. Scott.

"Those were the coordinates you gave me!"

"They were correct. I am apparently on an exact duplicate of the *Enterprise.*"

"What's that? Is it in orbit?"

"You could say so; Gideon is in orbit, this ship is on Gideon."

"Weel, that's a beginning, Spock. What about the Captain?"

"I'm sure he's somewhere here, Mr. Scott. I'm picking up life readings locally. Spock over and out."

Kirk knelt by the side of the bunk where Odona lay, flushed with fever, her cloud of silvery black hair tarnished and lifeless. He looked up at Hodin.

"If you do not let me get Dr. McCoy it will soon be too late for her."

"We have told you, Captain Kirk. It is her wish and mine that there be no interference with the natural development of this precious virus."

"What is the matter with you? If she lives, her blood would contain the virus just as mine does. She doesn't have to die."

"She must die. Our people must believe in this escape."

"She is so young . . ."

"Because she is young she will be an inspiration to our people. Don't you see, Captain, she will become a symbol for others to follow? In time, Gideon will once again be the Paradise it was . . ."

Odona's sigh pierced the shell of exaltation Hodin had erected around his consciousness. Kirk smoothed her blazing forehead; Hodin stood by her bedside in a state of misery. But Odona's weary eyes only gazed at Kirk.

"I . . . am glad you are here. Is my time short?"

"Very short," Kirk whispered.

"I asked you to make the journey last forever." She smiled wanly. "It began here, didn't it?"

Kirk spoke very clearly, hoping to penetrate the feverish haze that surrounded her senses.

"The journey can continue. If you will let me, I can make you well."

"Like your arm?"

He nodded hopefully. She lay still, expressionless. Then, with a slight cry, she raised her arms to embrace him. The delicacy that had given her such grace in health now gave her too much fragility in his arms. He willed her with all his might to agree to be cured.

"I am not afraid of ... what will happen. I am not at all afraid," she murmured feebly against his shoulder. "It's only that now ... I wish it could be ... with you ... forever ..." Her voice sank. Gently Kirk laid her unconscious head on the pillow.

The door closed with a decisive snap.

"I am glad to see you looking so well, Captain. Apparently Starfleet's analysis was correct after all." Spock's cool words cut into the air.

Kirk whirled; it *was* Spock. "I'm fine," he managed to say. "But we do have a patient." He lifted Odona from the bed. Hodin stood, paralyzed.

"Spockto*Enterprise* Spockto*Enterprise* Threetobeamup Mr.Scott," Spock slipped the words out with machine-gun speed.

"Three—? Er—same coordinates, Mr. Spock?"

Scott had obviously grasped the need for haste.

Hodin plunged at Spock with an inarticulate sound of fury.

"Your Excellency, please do not interfere." As the sparkles replaced the three figures, Mr. Spock's last, "I already have enough to explain to upper echelons, Prime Minister," hung in the air over Hodin's impotent rage.

"I am ... cured?" Odona's tone wavered between disappointment and wonder.

"Completely." Kirk lifted her to her feet and stood smiling down at her brightened eyes.

"Then I can now take your place on Gideon," she said gravely.

"Is that what you want to do?" Kirk was very

serious, yet a small smile crossed his face as he watched her. She touched his cheek tenderly, lightly.

"That is what I must do. I am needed there."

Kirk kissed her hand, a gesture of salute to her gallantry—and a farewell. "People like you are needed everywhere, Odona."

They walked side by side into the corridor.

"Will you sign this, please, sir?" A young crewman held out a clipboard to Kirk. He scrawled his initials, and in the bustle of traffic in the corridor he saw her watching a couple stroll hand in hand toward the lounge. As she caught his eye, the wistfulness in her face vanished. She smiled.

"It's different from our *Enterprise*."

"It's almost exactly the same," said Kirk. "Only this one works." He added wryly, "And it's crowded."

She laughed. "Does it seem so to you?"

"It does now."

"Excuse me, Captain, but before this young lady goes home we are obliged to devise some way to complete our mission. The Prime Minister, you may recall, was somewhat agitated when we last saw him." Spock was apologetic, but quite firm.

Kirk clapped a hand to his head. "Foof, I was forgetting him. Call McCoy and Scott; we'll confer on the bridge."

"Captain," said Spock very formally. "I beg leave to report that I have broken regulations. Starfleet Command gave specific orders which I, upon my own responsibility, disobeyed. In view of Prime Minister Hodin's intransigence to date . . ."

"If you mean father," said Odona, "he did not really want me to volunteer for this sickness at all. He will be grateful to have me back, and if I am carrying the virus, all will be well."

"He wanted you to be a symbol for your people," said Kirk thoughtfully. "He was quite impassioned about that, Odona."

"He had to have some way to live with himself, letting me die, Captain," said Odona gently. "I haven't died. Perhaps there may be some way to inspire our people, nevertheless."

Spock was frowning into his console. "I wonder," he said. "There are many ways to gather public approval—besides the sacrifice of . . . er . . . young women."

There was a silence; each of them cast about in his mind for alternatives. Hodin required something that would serve to call forth volunteers from his people for infection with a deadly disease; and this was a unique public relations problem for the crew of the *Enterprise* to consider.

"In the old days of medicine . . ." began McCoy. "I seem to recall that there was some sort of signal . . . illness aboard, doctor required; I don't quite remember . . ."

Spock laughed. "Bravo, Doctor!" He punched rapidly at his console. "Here it is; a distress flag, flown by seagoing vessels . . . the design sounds simple enough."

Uhura rose from her seat. "I'll see to it at once." She left the room quickly.

"What is it? What are you doing?" Odona was unable to follow their rapid trains of thought. Kirk smiled to himself. This time her puzzlement was genuine.

"What we propose, madame, is to send you home with a badge of honor," said Spock. "When you show it to your father, he can offer such badges to all your people who volunteer for the . . . service he so urgently wishes to render them. This will make it a matter of pride to have such a badge in the family, and thus serve the same purpose as your death was designed to do."

Uhura returned with a small flag, as described by Spock. Kirk took it from her, and going up to Odona, while the crew stood at full attention, he pinned it ceremoniously to her shoulder.

"For service to Gideon above and beyond the call of duty," he intoned. He hesitated, then kissed her on both cheeks. "An old custom of some of our people," he said, smiling at her blush.

"Will you stay on the ship?" she whispered.

He looked at her quickly. In that moment he recognized the ambiguity of her question, and replied unmistakably.

"On *this* ship, I will stay, Odona."

She said wistfully, "Forever?"

"Sometimes I think so," he said, very quietly. "But this is my ship, my dear." He struck at the intercom. "Kirk to Transporter Room. One to beam down to Gideon."

Later, McCoy asked, "Captain, is the Federation really all that anxious to gain the membership of what is now more or less a plague planet?"

"That," said Kirk, with a glance at Spock, "will be for the diplomats to decide."